DEAR CHRYSANTHEMUMS

A NOVEL IN STORIES

FIONA SZE-LORRAIN

SCRIBNER

NEW YORK   LONDON   TORONTO   SYDNEY   NEW DELHI

Scribner
An Imprint of Simon & Schuster, Inc.
1230 Avenue of the Americas
New York, NY 10020

Published by agreement with Agentur Nina Sillem, Frankfurt, Germany

First Scribner trade paperback edition May 2023

For information about special discounts for bulk purchases, please contact Simon & Schuster Special Sales at 1-866-506-1949 or business@simonandschuster.com.

The Simon & Schuster Speakers Bureau can bring authors to your live event. For more information or to book an event, contact the Simon & Schuster Speakers Bureau at 1-866-248-3049 or visit our website at www.simonspeakers.com.

Interior design by Jaime Putorti

Manufactured in the United States of America

1   3   5   7   9   10   8   6   4   2

Library of Congress Cataloging-in-Publication Data has been applied for.

ISBN 978-1-6680-1298-7
ISBN 978-1-6680-1300-7 (ebook)

for Christina
and for Susanna

Secrets on earth
thunder in heaven

A CHINESE FIGURE

CONTENTS

YI — MEANS ONE

The brush must turn inward once it touches rice paper. Hide its tip to temper the opening. To amend the fall. To move the ink across a page with an untamed brush. Trust water enough not to dilute the ink. So the word appears steady and more or less alive, like a x-rayed femur, before the stroke waxes outward and into a bridge, closer to a mist, the negative of a river, down a canyon across the wild temple, from smoke to white ashes, the spine of a folded moon, its ladder, and our spare table, a horizontal scroll that can never come to light, carried from one house to another village, a grave and torch missing, each open field ready for its name, a generation to outshine the previous and the next.

No pressure—point at a center.

The center stops. Its line does not break.

Let the character grow old in one breath.

I

Summer is here—
so says a spacious
newspaper ad

AFTER OZAKI HŌSAI

DEATH AT THE WUKANG MANSION

1966

Ling arrived at the Wukang Mansion a little past midnight. The stairways were bleak. Lights flickered. In spite of the silence, the subdued colors, every household seemed awake. The place felt restless. Barely a month had passed since the launch of the Cultural Revolution, and electricity was palpable in the air. Ling was assigned to unit 6, studio 42, on the third story of the northern wing. She'd come to Shanghai with a bag of clothes and few personal items. Despite what she'd heard about the building, she had not expected its imposing architecture. Sometimes it was a glowering king; other times it looked like a shabby tyrant who had lost track of his followers. From a distance she gasped at it, even before turning onto the main boulevard.

When Ling arrived at her unit, she noticed a spacious room next to her studio. It was unoccupied. She entered her studio gingerly and was taken aback by the spartan neatness: the bedroom had been carved from a once-larger apartment. A bed, a side table, a desk, a chair, made of wood and without character. Even so, in those days, it could have housed a working-class family of five or six. No one told her anything beforehand—not even Deputy

Director Shao, who assigned her the unit and hired her for a local drama troupe before it was shut down. But Ling knew from the stillness and the musty smell. There was a coffin inside.

The corridors were cramped with pots and pans, piles of newspapers, and chaotic columns of cardboard boxes. Singlets, blouses, and pants were drying on racks and wires that zigzagged haphazardly across one another in midair. The place smelled of charcoal, leek, and damp bricks. The odor of ruins jolted Ling out of her imagination, the fabulous Wukang Mansion from the roaring twenties. Once in a while, a shuffle of footsteps, followed by hushed tones, came from above or below. A basin dropped and a child bawled; kitchen utensils clinked and clanged against one another.

The coffin arrived early each morning, before Ling stepped out at eight to buy breakfast—a cheap fried dough stick or tea egg—from a stall vendor across the street. For the rest of the day, the coffin stayed where it was. Shortly after the evening radio news broadcast at six, a group of young Red Guards would come to claim their prize.

By the end of her first week, Ling had learned the routine by heart: how the coffin left the building after being shouldered down the stairs by three stone-faced teenagers who struggled with each step. Through the servants' quarters south of her block, it entered a backyard crowded with potted plants. Hoarse yells of political slogans resonated through the corridors amidst boisterous gesticulations from residents observing from higher floors. The coffin came without a lid.

No one wept. No one bothered with gossip. It was as practical as that: a rectangular box made of four light wooden planks and a base. Come morning, the same coffin was returned to the same room, either empty or carrying a new body, again dragged up each flight of stairs and without affect, though ironically, with more swiftness, more wariness, and this time, by the concierge Old Dan and his wife.

Day in, day out, the coffin came and went, efficiently and without fail, like the glorious sun that rose in the east but never set in the west in every revolutionary song or ode, which all patriots of a New China must memorize and praise. Everyone in the Wukang Mansion seemed determined to keep out of one another's way and avoid one another's gaze, especially Old Dan, who was hard of hearing and never greeted a new tenant. His wife couldn't stop complaining in her peculiar accent that added an *er* sound to almost every word, "Tenants these days never last through the winter." She did not sound like a native of Shanghai.

But the retired couple were now concierges in name only. Other than carrying the coffin, they no longer bore any responsibility or collective duties, let alone cared for the maintenance of this eight-story building, nearly a hundred cramped units, littered with stains, cracks, and messy *dazibao*, big-character posters in black and red ink that were torn off or pasted over their notoriously long and damp corridor walls. On a peeling wall outside Ling's studio, excerpts from the great

Chinese classic novel *The Water Margin* were inscribed like graffiti, in clusters of tiny, squeezed characters in cursive. From afar they looked like rectangular hills of ants. The novel narrated the historical fiction of one hundred and eight outlaws during the Northern Song era. These legendary outlaws fought and defended their Chinese lands against the nomadic Khitan invaders, but they died on the battlefield or were summoned to court, betrayed by their own emperor.

Now and then Ling kept her door ajar, not to engage in small talk with passersby, but hoping to steal a peek at the face inside the coffin. On some days, the body was shrouded in a dirty white blanket. On other days, a few spread-out sheets of used newspapers covered the face. In the end, it was the faces of the tall, waiflike Red Guards she couldn't erase from her mind before she slept. In their shrill voices, they sang in off-pitch prophetic refrains from the theme song of the model ballet opera *The Red Detachment of Women*. They sang with gusto, without regard for tenants in the building or for the early morning hour:

> *Forward! Forward!*
> *How heavy the soldiers' responsibility,*
> *How deep the hatred of women runs!*

When they marched, they looked straight ahead, heads slightly tilted up to the left, without even a blink. Once the coffin dropped from their hands and to the floor. It slid down a flight with a thud when one of the Red Guards missed a step. Ling rushed out her door. Stunned by such a dramatic descent of the coffin and their apparent helplessness, the Red Guards scrambled down the stairs, put their hands to their faces, and shrieked, as if screaming for their own lives, and it was only then that Ling realized, curbing her thrill, that they were not young men at all—they were girls who hadn't yet reached puberty.

Originally the Normandie Apartments, the Wukang Mansion was designed and built in 1924 by the Hungarian Slovak architect László Hudec, who as a prisoner of war landed in Shanghai in 1918 after fleeing from a camp in Siberia. Myth has it that he jumped off a train and made his way by foot to the Paris of the East. Located at the juncture of two major streets lined with plane trees, Wukang Road and Huaihai Middle Road, joined by four other roads in the former French Concession, the Wukang Mansion was a lofty eight-story building. It featured the architectural style of the French Renaissance. In the shape of a battleship of the Normandie class during the first World War—this was probably how its actual name came about—the Wukang Mansion could be seen right down the ends of the pair of intersecting streets, towering at a height of thirty meters over an area of more than nine thousand square meters, with balconies on both sides of its wedge and an open-air compound at the top.

Ling had read about the building's illustrious history. During her conservatory years, she had fantasized about living there. Home to affluent foreigners during the twenties and later, during the last Republican years, some of the most celebrated film and entertainment luminaries, patrons, and literati of Big Shanghai, the Wukang Mansion boasted arcades, spiral stairways, intricately tiled walls, vaults, elevators, modern facilities, Art Deco features, and needless to say, its international cultural setting and sophisticated social ambience. It wasn't just classy, it was operatic. The lesbian daughter of the wealthiest banker of China, Dr. H. H. Kung, purchased the building after the Sino-Japanese War and built for herself an opulent garden and swimming pool on the second floor before fleeing to Taiwan. Ling could understand why the place was now considered "anti-revisionist," a target for the nascent Cultural Revolution. Soon after the movement's first wave of purges, the raging red summer, the Flatiron Building of Shanghai was nicknamed the "diving pool of Shanghai," where intellectuals and celebrities accused of being counterrevolutionaries plunged to their death from the roof.

One Sunday afternoon, Ling was doing her laundry in the communal kitchen basin, down the westerly corridor on the second story. The old cast-iron sink stank of sewage and pipes. Ling tried not to lean against the rusty basin, where dirt, hair, and food waste collected. The stopper was moldy. It attracted moth flies. She was hand-washing her undergarments under a running tap when Old Dan's wife ran up from the backyard.

"Comrade, you have a visitor." Old Dan's wife was panting. "She is there now . . . waiting in your apartment."

Old Dan's wife was expecting Ling to ask who, but the question never came. She stood at the entrance, mouth agape.

Ling dropped her cake of soap, startled. She dried her hands in her pockets and on the back of her pants. Looking up into the extended horizontal mirror that hung angled against the ceiling, she unrolled the ends of her sleeves. As she adjusted her blue Mao suit, she saw in the mirror, from the corner of her eye, how Old Dan's wife looked back twice furtively behind her, like a thief, before disappearing down the aisle. What was wrong with this old woman? Why did she spy, and why was she so lousy at hiding it? Still, none of the old woman's comic awkwardness distracted Ling as much as offended or worried her, as her heart skipped a beat and she speculated about Comrade Shao's motives for showing up without notice.

But when Ling pulled back the curtain door and stepped into the studio, she was cheerful. She put on a set smile. "Welcome, Comrade Shao! I didn't know you planned to drop by today." She tried to sound normal and optimistic. "I would have prepared some noodles and fruit. Would you like something?"

Deputy Director Shao stood at the window, looking out on Huaihai Road, her hands behind her back. From there, she could see the private residence and garden of the esteemed political figure Soong Ching-ling—the wife of Sun Yat-sen, the "Father of Republican China," and the elder sister of Madame Chiang Kai-shek. Soong Ching-ling was the last of the distinguished Soong family to remain in Communist China. Could it have been any more coincidental that the lesbian daughter of Kung the banker who was once a celebrity tenant of the Wukang Mansion was also a niece of Soong Ching-ling through Soong's and Madame Chiang's eldest sister, Kung's wife? In a corner right outside Soong's compound was the stall vendor who sold Ling tea eggs and fried dough sticks, squatting in the heat under a floppy straw hat.

Deputy Director Shao turned around and smiled at Ling. Her glasses perched low on her nose; she pushed them up and looked meaningfully at Ling. Poised, like a teacher staring down at a student who has lost her tongue, she appeared taller and much more muscular than Ling had expected. Her skin was tanned and she sported a short "liberation" bob. She was clad in the typical green Mao soldier shirt and wrinkled pants, all of which contributed to her stern, masculine demeanor. Even a cadre or a peasant must appear reformed.

"Please, Comrade Shao, have a seat and make yourself at home."

Ling moved a chair to the table next to the wall. She poured tea from a peony-covered thermos on the table and served Shao a cup. The tea was lukewarm. Ling stood like a sentry. She smiled to hide her anxiety.

"How are things coming along here?" Shao asked as she scanned the apartment without concealing her intent. "I hope the Wukang Mansion suits you. Everyone has a story to tell about this place. You must be settled down by now, I'm assuming."

"Yes, of course," Ling mumbled.

Nothing had happened so far anyway, she almost uttered out loud instead of under her breath. Apart from buying herself breakfast and getting groceries, Ling had indeed done nothing but stay put in her room. In the mornings, when the stall vendor asked how she was, she responded that the day had not yet begun. After breakfast, she tuned in to the radio for whatever news she could get. By then, loudspeakers atop the building were broadcasting Mao's writings and the proceedings of struggle sessions against class enemies from other cities.

The broadcast voices drummed into Ling's head. Often she tried to read a few pamphlets and a dusty copy of Lu Xun's *Diary of a Madman* that she stumbled upon while rummaging a low cupboard near the door. But several pages were torn off those scant publications, and Ling found it hard to concentrate after a while. When she shut her eyes, she visualized each character being burned into her skin by a searing branding iron, one followed by another. In cold sweat, she squealed and woke up, only to realize that it was a nightmare, even though she had only been half-asleep in her chair, next to feverish voices from the portable radio.

In the afternoons, Ling stretched her body in her room, doing some basic dance steps such as pliés, standing en pointe, and working on splits. Just to maintain grace, as her teacher used to advise her. She practiced turning around without the faintest sound or quiver in the air, and when she leapt, she hummed the beginning of *Swan Lake*'s overture and scissored her steps rhythmically, before trying on sequences of sautés, then some small jetés. By now she had to have been one of the few of her generation who knew the music in and out from *Swan Lake*. Ling's teacher used to praise her for her discipline and elegance, and she remembered all too well how her lithe figure appeared in the mirror of the dance classroom, a space converted from a Ping-Pong room with a roof that leaked in a village school . . . But Ling must now execute these moves discreetly, for fear of being denounced for her capitalist dance exercises. Move as naturally as possible, she murmured, and set the bar higher for herself: be lighter than air. When all else failed, she tried to write her confession—she did not forget about it, of course—but could never get past half a sheet of those red square manuscript papers that would forever follow her in a file somewhere and determine the rest of her life and sufferings.

*

Day in, day out, Ling had waited for someone to contact her. The streets outside the Wukang Mansion buzzed with commotion on top of its daily bustle. Hordes of Red Guards and angry workers paraded "radical elements," denouncing them late into the night. Shanghai was awash with the revolution. Yet Ling had not expected her own deputy director to show up in person.

"I'm ready for work." Ling cleared her throat. "I know my limits and I confess my errors. Is there anything I can do to serve the people?"

"What would you like to do?" Shao asked, raising her voice.

Ling detected a shade of mockery. The deputy director took out a Zhongnanhai cigarette from her pocket—one of the most exclusive cigarettes specially manufactured to honor Chairman Mao—and put it on the table. "Still dreaming of becoming a Hollywood star? Or hoping to outshine Madame Mao one day?"

"Er . . . I could teach an evening class or . . . I could lead a Chairman Mao Thought reading group for our factory workers . . . in the neighborhood, the Xuhui District. Long live . . . long live the Revolution," Ling stammered, her head bowed. It was clear that she was a lamb before slaughter, scared out of her wits. What else could the poor girl say to plead her case? Standing all the while against the cupboard, Ling wrapped her arms around herself, as if on the verge of being stripped naked.

"I guess, I guess . . . I can't act or perform in public anymore, can I?" Her voice trembled.

"*Well* . . . that depends," responded Shao deliberately, as she began to play with the cigarette with her left thumb and index finger. Sitting with legs crossed, the deputy director swung her right leg brazenly and asked, "So, have you been going out into the city of late?"

Ling shook her head. She had been dreading this question since she first arrived. Shao must be here to grill her until she sprouted nonsense, denounced someone, or confessed whatever Shao wanted. Somehow she knew these interrogations would occur over and over again, not just in a cell, but anywhere now. She would be stopped by anyone, anytime, even where she was living. Yes, right here, in the Wukang Mansion. Hadn't she proven her guilt during those purge sessions before coming to Shanghai? Hadn't she been humiliated enough?

Shao leaned forward and probed again, raising her voice slightly. As if to prepare Ling for the worst, she squinted and hardened her gaze. "Any contact with your family or former friends of late?"

Again Ling shook her head, still bowed. She shuddered without restraint but controlled the tears at the back of her eyes. She thought of her husband—now ex-husband—Little Bao, an electrician back home in Hangzhou. Oh, how he'd doted on Ling before her deceitful behavior came out. He must have been a broken man now, or who knows, have taken a new wife, younger and prettier. Little Bao was an honest lad, yes, illiterate, but he had treated her like a jewel until . . .

"There is a price to pay for being different and desired," Shao touted with confidence. "Luckily for you, someone high up was kind enough to protect you, and you were transferred to Shanghai. So here you are, safe and sound!"

"Your looks and body, your talents on the silver screen have protected you so far, but adultery is one of the worst crimes in our socialist world. Imagine if someone reported you to a friend of Madame Mao, goodness knows where you would be locked up. You know what the guards will do to you in those places. Worse, you aren't just a bitch who made your husband a cuckold, you have even seduced young women and sucked their nipples and toes!"

Ling burst into tears. How hopeless and indecent she felt in this filthy body that had once brought applause and gawking from admirers nationwide. She dug her fingernails into her own arms. As she cried, spasms of pain nabbed her abdomen. Why couldn't she vanish into thin air? What must she do to get out of this wretched body and place? Thoughts raced in her head as she grew more distressed in Shao's presence. Ling buried her face in her hands in shame. At that point, she realized that she had forgotten her undergarments in a soup bowl in the communal kitchen sink. In no time, she imagined, even residents in the Wukang Mansion would know all about her previous life. She would be paraded with her hair shaved and stoned in public. She imagined mothers, wives, and daughters scorning her, eager to skin her alive, while fathers, husbands, and sons gave her kicks in succession, calling her the worst names, as she staggered past their beastly gazes. The scenes replayed themselves in slow motion, and anguish seized Ling's throat until she nearly couldn't breathe.

Ling's heart was beating faster. She thought of those Red Guard girls, this time pointing their fingers in her face and accusing her before the crowd in front of the Wukang Mansion, of how she had been watching them and lusting after their bodies every morning when they came for the coffin next door . . .

"Oh, my sweet pea, don't cry your heart out." Shao's voice softened, but her gaze continued to pierce through Ling. She got up and approached Ling, who was shaking. "So you like women, huh?" The deputy director grinned and lowered her voice to a whisper. "Well, we need to think of a good way to fix that problem here in Shanghai . . . What do you think?"

Steadily, as if to console the shaky Ling, Shao removed Ling's hands over her face. She put a finger beneath Ling's chin and stroked it. She blew mildly at her finger and Ling's chin. While she tried to get Ling to look up into her eyes, she placed her other hand over one of Ling's breasts and shook it. She wasn't gentle, but not violent enough for Ling to make a scene. Her hands firm on Ling's breast, Shao closed her eyes, adjusted her feet clumsily with knees bent, and started to make herself come.

Ling moaned. She felt wet too—she was aroused. Her chest burned and tightened, its heart draining off under the weight of fresh bricks from a furnace in each lung, one stacked atop another, on and on. It was pumping too hard. The world picked up speed. Ling's eyes blurred. She began to gasp for air.

"We should have brought her some pancakes or soup. You could have asked her round for tea," muttered Old Dan as he closed Ling's eyelids. "What has she been doing all this while, locked up on her own in this apartment?"

"Don't be dumb. It wasn't possible . . . You know that better than anyone else here. They've been watching her closely even from afar," scolded his wife. "Sometimes I wonder if she was a spy. Holed up in her room, she must have been up to something nasty. The way she looked at me askew was so creepy. Her bourgeois habits and lifestyle . . . Look at this studio, sparse and luminous, and how she's decorated it." The place looked banal, but its minimalism spoke of a presence. Old Dan's wife pointed to a ripped landscape painting scroll, taped back into a piece on the wall next to Ling's bed. Most people would have hung a colored copy of Chairman Mao's portrait or some propaganda poster in its place. A jade-green vase without a design motif was placed on a nightstand, next to Ling's embroidered floral handkerchief. A Mao alarm clock ticked away. These were some of Ling's few personal belongings that had counted down her final days.

"I wish we'd done something." Old Dan shook his head. "After all, she didn't give us trouble like the other girls. At least we could have talked to her and made her feel at ease. Shouldn't we find someone to contact her family before reporting to her deputy director? Where does she come from? And where exactly is her family? I overheard Suzhou or Nanjing . . ."

"No point in having regrets, old man," said his wife. "What can ordinary people like us do? Better to play safe than to pay the price—"

"I know . . . Who can tell what will become of our great proletariat revolution. What may tomorrow bring us?"

"Poor thing. I wonder what she knew before moving in. This apartment is jinxed, I know it! Surely she must have discovered in the weeks after her move, every other actress who stayed here ended up taking her life."

"But not the way she did . . . Fortunately for us, and for herself, there was no mess, no blood lying around. She died a natural death, all right, but we the living must continue to survive with this never-ending curse here at our good old Wukang Mansion. We might as well work at a morgue for the rest of our lives. At least we've found her on the floor in her room, but when could that have happened?" Perplexed and defeated, Old Dan took a deep breath. Just as he was about to heave a sigh, his wife raised her eyebrows, put a finger to her lips, then pointed it to the ceiling, as if someone had been eavesdropping on them all along.

Old Dan paused and stared at his wife. He nodded. Quickly, he motioned her to carry Ling's body by her feet while grabbing her upper body by its shoulders. He touched Ling's bony frame and felt it right away. It surprised him that despite its slender build, the young woman's body, once limber, sank with a mass and weight as onerous as the anonymous others he lifted and carried down the stairs every day. *Moving the dead is less a burden than inciting the living to action, as long as death doesn't drag its feet,* he reminded himself, quoting a timeworn adage from his hometown village on the outskirts of Shanghai, and looked up to check if his wife was coping fine with Ling's legs.

Foam oozed from both corners of Ling's lips. Like a faithful servant, Old Dan wiped it off with the back of his calloused right hand. He almost wanted to ask her for forgiveness. But as his wife had bluntly put it, it was too late for regrets: When and who should he start with, anyway, if he searched for redemption? How many bodies had he shoved away without caring who the dead were or what they'd done? The proverb *Do not judge a life until the man's coffin is closed* came to Old Dan. What bullshit, how contradictory the Chinese language. We use a coffin with no lid and it cannot be closed. Old Dan caressed Ling's cheeks. She was an orphan who did not belong to this place. Youth was dark, its promises brutal. Passion turned out to be more political than calamitous, less tempestuous than deviant, for better or for worse, without exception.

By that point Ling's face had stiffened and turned cold and ashen gray, but Old Dan could touch the silkiness of its almost perfect skin. She must have been a classical dancer before becoming an actress, he muttered to himself. She was probably one of the best in the province. No matter what, he reckoned, they must move her to the coffin in the next room before he phoned her deputy director. Tomorrow, Old Dan thought again and without a doubt, an ordinary summer day in 1966, the Year of the Fire Horse, an all-girl company of Red Guards would come for Ling. Their fists clenched and heads tilted to the left, they would carry the coffin out of the mansion, led by Deputy Director Shao, who would inspect the studio before sending over someone new.

II

while I'm being watched
it's hard to spit out
watermelon seeds

INAHATA TEIKO

COOKING FOR MADAME CHIANG

1946

O f course I can make red-braised pork and scallion pancakes," Chang'er told the head housekeeper. "Who can't in Shanghai?"

But that was the point: she was no longer in Shanghai, her hometown. Separated for months from her husband Tao, and with no news of his whereabouts, Chang'er needed work to save herself—at least until the civil war ended.

Chang'er smiled at the chief housekeeper, Old Yong, and patted her own chest. "I can also prepare lotus leaf rice," she said. "Or the famous Nanjing saltwater duck, wontons, soup dumplings, cabbage and pork rice cake . . . any southern food that Madame desires." Chang'er wanted to list every dish she knew, as if her culinary experience were a war medal to be displayed with pride.

"That is what I need to clarify from the outset," Old Yong said, then cleared his throat. "We want to hire you to make simple food for Madame's private meals, not for banquets or family gatherings. You will be Madame's personal cook." Clad in a navy blue Chinese tunic and pants, the bald Old Yong carried himself with an air of dignity. He touched his thin moustache, stared at Chang'er, and continued, "In such times, we too have to cut our budget for lavish meals."

Chang'er bit her lip and kept quiet. She regretted having come across as overly enthusiastic. One must not be too desperate even when starving, Tao reprimanded her on the morning he had to pass by the harbor. That night he did not return. He never did. A neighbor from down their alley whispered into Chang'er's ears that Tao had gone underground to fight for the country—but truly, who could she trust? In troubled times, no one knew anything or anyone for certain. Even her own husband chose not to confide in her. She didn't even know if Tao sided with the Nationalists or the Communists.

Frowning down at her shoes, Chang'er fidgeted with her fingers one over another, her arms crossed behind her back.

Old Yong continued. "Can you make something called *sela*?"

Chang'er was bewildered. *Se-la*?

They stood in a private outer courtyard behind a red front gate, enclosed by beds of lilies, peonies, and tea olives, lined with neat rows of young wutong trees. At the rear of the compound stood a second gate to the main wing and residence halls and courtyards, each styled in the traditional architecture of a Chinese quadrangle compound that'd been in existence for dynasties.

Curious as ever, Chang'er peered over Old Yong's shoulders, distracted by the conspicuous serenity of the compound—the surrealism of it all, away from the babel and clamor of hungry war-stricken folks in the streets. This was, to her, paradise, a tranquil life in such a sterling hutong compound, sheltered and out of sight, deep in the heart of the city of Nanjing. Chang'er felt her body shrink in the best clothes she had brought. She felt small. Provincial too. Never had she once seen such extravagance in a private residence, not even in her Shanghai. Who was the family, her potential employer?

Old Yong followed Chang'er's gaze, then snorted knowingly, as if to ridicule the young woman's amazement, and asked again insistently, "So do you know how to make *sela*? It's supposed to be a Western cold dish. A starter, I presume. But our Madame prefers to eat light, so on occasion she requests it as a main dish. Especially for dinner. Or as a lunch snack, if she wakes up late after returning from trips. Either a *sela* with vegetables or a Chinese potato *sela* with a few sliced sausages and peas . . ."

"Oh, *sela*, yes, sure! Of course I can make a *sela*, a potato salad," Chang'er said hastily, with delight in her voice, like an overjoyed child's.

Old Yong's eyes widened as Chang'er chattered away, showing off. The Shanghainese had long been touted for their cosmopolitan outlook, fashion, vanity, and "foreign" tastes—whatever *vain* or *foreign* might connote—not to mention their splurge, arrogance, drama, and insufferable sense of superiority. Maybe Chang'er hadn't been entirely immune.

"Anyone in Shanghai knows how to make a Shanghai *sela*! That isn't just a Western dish. Very convenient . . . no big deal for a cook. I can make a *sela* for Madame's lunch, keep the leftovers for her dinner or snacks.

"You can serve them with our classic cold sesame noodles. Thin noodles, I mean—I can make those too. We Shanghainese are known for our unparalleled potato salad. We learned from the Russians and their original Olivier salad. Does Madame like it plain with sesame oil or with a light spicy flavor? I can sprinkle in bits and pieces of tomato, turnip, carrot, onion, ginger, cucumber . . . or thin wedges of cooked ham. If I may, I'll add diced apple and slices of bamboo shoots with cilantro."

This was more than enough information for Old Yong, who nodded and flashed Chang'er a toothless smile. He saw no need to reveal to Chang'er that their Madame, like Chang'er herself, hailed from Shanghai, and in spite of her years growing up in America, had become nostalgic of late for her hometown food. He then straightened his face and set forth what seemed to be his final condition. "Of course you must not tell anyone that you are cooking for Madame Chiang Kai-shek."

So it was neither the reputed Nanjing saltwater duck, nor the clay pot of braised tofu and mushrooms, nor the acclaimed dessert soup of glutinous rice balls with black sesame and red bean paste fillings, nor any sumptuous delicacy from the south that Chang'er prepared in the first week of work in Madame Chiang's household. When she arrived at six each morning, she was greeted not by Old Yong, but by Madame Chiang's personal helper, Little Green. She waited for Chang'er at the front gate and guided her to the kitchen in one of the side wings.

Some ten years older than Chang'er, Little Green had a mole that sat conspicuously below her lips. That first day, she dressed simply but smartly, in a salmon-pink cotton blouse with long sleeves and checkered duck-blue pants. She walked briskly, two braids swinging over her shoulders, and hummed a folk tune. A white handkerchief was tucked at the top frog button of her blouse, near its mandarin collar. Without ado, she showed Chang'er around the kitchen.

Tucked in one of the northern wings, separate from the common courtyards, the cooking space was immaculate and organized: several wooden tables, old-fashioned Chinese pantries, and stoves, as well as pots, woks, bowls, and plates of all sizes and types stacked in neat rows on long benches and stools against the walls. A slow fire crackled off at the firewood in a corner of the kitchen. The place was chilly. Drafts of cold air rushed in and out, a far cry from the oily or steamy southern kitchen that Chang'er had known since she was a child. The tables, however, were heaped with food: peaches, pears, apples, spinach, small Chinese cabbages, two chickens ready to be plucked and skinned, and a few baskets of eggs, under which sacks of rice and flour were kept alongside more baskets and jars of sorghum wine.

"You aren't responsible for getting the ingredients. Our housemaids will buy the fresh stock. You'll be told what to cook when you arrive." Little Green pointed to two tin pails at the doorway and instructed Chang'er to steam two buckets of milk or soybean milk first thing when she reported every morning.

"Whatever for?" Chang'er blurted with a chortle. "That's quite a lot of milk, don't you think? Madame Chiang would be farting or burping from dawn to dusk!"

Little Green stopped short and glared at Chang'er. She looked around to be sure that they were free from prying eyes. Then she snapped, "You're no different from the others. I thought you came from Shanghai, so aren't you a clever girl? As it turns out, even at eighteen, your brain is as opaque as a wooden block! Madame Chiang doesn't drink this milk, don't you get it?"

Chang'er shrugged, nonplussed. How was she supposed to know what Little Green meant?

"Every morning, before dressing up for the day and putting on makeup, Madame Chiang washes her face with milk," Little

Green explained calmly. She raised her eyebrows, rolled her eyes, and said, "That's her morning ritual, and ours too. We keep this precious milk in that corner, see?"

Before leaving Chang'er to the kitchen, Little Green elaborated. "Once or twice a week, we leave the milk—or soybean milk—in our backyard. Let it solidify gradually. Not to the point of freezing it, though. Just enough for Madame Chiang to use as a night facial mask. Generally, Madame Chiang likes it close to a delicate gauze. In summer, it gets too hot even in the evening. So we use bean curd."

A large oval wooden tub with a lid waited on the kitchen table for Chang'er. The young cook blushed. She opened her mouth with disbelief. Milk and beans for proteins had become such a luxury, a scarcity during the war years. Desperate mothers begged and scrambled to find milk for their newborn babies, but to wash one's face *every day* with milk for beauty purposes was virtually unheard of, even for a Shanghainese with some years of school like herself. How did Madame Chiang's household manage to secure such an abundance of milk? The black market, no doubt . . . or was the milk imported? Chang'er opened the lid. She eyed the white viscous liquid in the dim morning light. Strangely, it looked more like frozen latex or cooked glue, or a round white fabric.

Chang'er rolled up her right sleeve, revealing the brown sickle scar on her right forearm. It slanted across her skin like an implanted piece of rope. It wasn't a burn or an accident or something that she was born with, yet she was destined to bear it as long as she lived: a disfigured creature on her arm that repelled kindness and fortune. What could she do to scrape it off her skin?

From the wooden tub, Chang'er dished out a cup of milk, ready to scoop out more and empty it into a bigger basin and to heat the milk over the furnace behind a crimson-red pantry. Cautiously she inhaled, and like a greedy child, she dipped a finger into the cold milk and rubbed it fast against her scar. She did it as rigorously as she could. If Madame Chiang had applied it warm over her face for a skin-care routine, what was the harm in trying cold milk on her own flaw? If the milk wouldn't remove the scar, maybe it would at least improve the look of it. She rubbed it clockwise for a few min-utes and counted to a hundred before licking and washing her arm. Her tongue tasted not sweetness as she had anticipated, but a sour and tingling sensation, a sharpness that reminded her of brambles and jagged grass scratching her legs when she ran in the meadows with the family dog. Who cares? Sooner or later, maybe her skin would be as smooth and porcelain white as Madame Chiang's.

Under the glacial tap water, Chang'er's arm sensed a crispness that vibrated like a wave. It was the touch of her husband, who enjoyed caressing her neck at the end of the day, before they made love and fell asleep. They'd married when Chang'er turned fifteen. Since, the bride had learned to live with the unspoken. Whenever Tao returned late with bloodstained hands—in the dark he franti-cally washed them in a pail—Chang'er pretended she saw nothing. She cleaned his clothes as if the blood on them were a soulless animal's. Three years into their marriage, she had yet to bear Tao a child. No one gossiped, but Chang'er was conscious of hostile talk. She grew uneasy. For some inexplicable reason, she now attributed her infertility to this scar, a curse that separated her from love and a smooth life—how it meandered and came alive like a snake spirit whenever she felt lonely, while in a revamped life, her affectionate husband Tao, who kept mum about his clandestine involvement with local guerrillas, would fondle and stroke it at night, not minding in the least her childlessness and their lack of a future together.

But one day—Chang'er was certain about her hunch—this scar would disappear. She couldn't stop missing Tao and worrying for him, and though she had never dared to believe in luck, she believed in it now. It was luck, perhaps, that had brought her to this kitchen, this fountain of healing milk.

So this was what she did the first thing each morning that she worked in Madame Chiang's kitchen: she bathed her scar with milk that Madame Chiang used as daily facial wash. Readying herself to pray for a child, Chang'er rubbed her arm piously with milk from the wooden tub, layer by layer around the scar. As the milk breezed along her arm, skipping breakfast to feel mortal, she dreamed of a better world. With time, this unsightly scar would fade—and on the day it blanched and vanished without her even realizing it, her beloved Tao would return.

As far as Chang'er was aware, Little Green never checked on her while she worked alone in the kitchen of the northern wing—and like Little Green, she hummed a pleasing tune or two. Neither did Old Yong, who eventually allowed her to surprise Madame Chiang with more elaborate dishes and sweetmeats besides the Shanghainese *sela* that Chang'er was required to cook. Time was the ingredient she blended each day into Madame Chiang's food. Time was an invisible hand to heal her scar with milk preserved for her mistress's beauty care. Milk and time. These were Chang'er's talismans. These were her secrets.

GREEN

1966

Last night, I dreamed of Chang'er standing at the entrance gate, as if she were again arriving for the first time at Madame Chiang's residence in Nanjing. In a blue padded robe, with a small, tattered brown suitcase beside her, she waved to me. From the south wing of the mansion, I was close enough to catch a glimpse of her tall silhouette, but not her face and short bangs, and I mistook her luggage for a dog.

But in reality her valise was empty, as I learned early on. "With such a smart prop, I must have come across as more convincing," Chang'er said to me a few days after she was hired. "I'm a professional." She jiggled her shoulders, two pigtails dangling. "Doesn't life seem like a film?" she added. "I must have looked as if I was going to work at the grand Cathay Hotel!"

What a child, I grumbled, holding back the urge to scold her. I couldn't help but want to be maternal. Her theatrical stunt—or shall I say, silliness—was typical of a coy Shanghainese girl who knew how to flirt and dress well, a charmer tilting her head, pouting, not necessarily to draw attention to herself, but more for the kick of creating a scene, making mischief. We tended to think of the Shanghainese as mean, but what did meanness stand for? How grand could they be when seeking work in the less glamorous Nanjing?

Old Yong stood at the door. He held a long conference with Chang'er—shaking his head and gesturing with his left arm and loose sleeve, the other hand behind his back, seemingly impatient—right there in the courtyard, without an umbrella, while it drizzled. He hired her on the spot. None of us servants eavesdropped on them, least of all me. No one would have imagined that she was the one our caretaker had been looking for all winter.

I did not expect Chang'er to help me out with Madame Chiang's formal meals—they were lavish and required experience in preparation—or her Wednesday tea sessions with American journalists and businessmen and her oldest sister, Nancy. Nor was Chang'er obliged to accompany me to the vegetable market and bargain with alley vendors on the way for the essentials. She wasn't even supposed to be Madame Chiang's personal cook, or so I was told at the beginning, but since she was tasked with making Madame Chiang's *sela*, I was more than glad to have her around, helping me prepare whatever light meals or snacks our mistress took on her own. Old Yong did not object, either.

What a relief. Until then, no one in the household had ever enjoyed making this bizarre cold dish. How on earth could anyone be expected to know it? Several times our enthused Madame Chiang described to Old Yong and me her nourishing *sela* in broad but ambiguous terms while showing us a black-and-white magazine clip with a recipe in some alien language.

Didn't it seem no more than a few slices of potatoes and raw carrots on a saucer? What about the sauce? Or was it some kind of corn paste?

Outside of the residence compound, I asked around for help. I tried to be discreet, but in vain. Even Shao, a middle school teacher who on occasion helped Madame Chiang acquire books from Confucius and Company at Taiping South Road, was curious: Why didn't Madame Chiang ask me to help her look it up? There are a few stacks of books on gastronomy in the municipal library archives. Isn't *sela* none other than a simple salad?

Of course not. I shook my head and waved my hand. And the sauce was certainly not your average black market soy sauce. Nor was it the sticky mayonnaise that a former servant of a British couple had once shared with me in secret. What if I had sprinkled some boiled peanuts into the chilled pork broth from one of Generalissimo Chiang's lunches, mixing it in with shreds of tapioca, radish, and shallot?

No one could figure the sauce out, so never once was Madame Chiang satisfied with the ever-evolving versions of *sela* that Old Yong and I had improvised. On her more tolerant days, she raised her eyebrows and vaguely twitched her lips. After taking a morsel, she heaved a quiet sigh and shook her index finger to indicate no.

But the first time Old Yong and I served her the *sela* prepared by Chang'er, Madame Chiang took a spoonful and blew at it.

"Clear and cool as a gust of autumn," she said in a hushed voice, as if reciting a verse.

Old Yong and I hung our heads and waited for the verdict. She leaned forward in her high-backed chair. I fiddled with a frayed thread from the hem of my blouse. Old Yong tried to hide his nerves. Madame Chiang looked up and cast us a sharp gaze, then softened her face and smiled.

"But, Sister Green, you got it all wrong," Chang'er squeaked, her hands fluttering around her head to dramatize the importance of what she had to say. "*Sela* isn't American. It's a Russian specialty and very much Shanghainese in every way!"

That was the first thing the girl said to me when I shuffled into the kitchen with Madame Chiang's empty saucer. I couldn't know if I was excited or bewildered, but my beaming face must have given me away. Madame Chiang had eaten all the *sela* and was even hoping for a second serving.

A second helping was almost unheard of. Our mistress was obsessed with her looks more than anything else, apart from her twice-daily milk bath and quick massage before her nap. She weighed herself every other day and ate like a bird. Even during the war, she took great pains to maintain her poise and figure. Since her marriage to the Generalissimo, our master tailor never saw the need to adjust her cheongsams. "Her waistline hasn't altered an inch," he exclaimed to us over and again in his high-pitched voice, like a strained tune from an opera aria.

Over time, I taught Chang'er to prepare our mistress's soya bean milk, and she started to help me with a variety of chores: skin the chickens; rinse fava beans, eggplants, and noodles; simmer pork loins over slow heat; and wash white fungi in salted water. I also taught her the Generalissimo's favorite taro soup. Her deft fingers danced whenever she made Madame Chiang's famous *sela*.

"Sugar is the secret," she whispered with a gleam in her right eye. "It doesn't matter if you soak the mixture of diced vegetables in sesame oil or in spicy broth. Always shower them with a dose of brown sugar." She rubbed her blind left eye with the back of her hand. "Ah, and never forget two tablespoons of Shaoxing wine. Sugar and wine—they make life bearable for us all."

It did not take Chang'er long to start pestering me for the secrets about Madame Chiang's skin-care routine: How long does Madame let the milk cool on her face? Does she powder it right after rinsing the milk off? Can the milk clog on its own? How long does it take to congeal into a mask over her face? Does it really improve her complexion? Should I rub it as herbal ointment on my left eye? One question after another.

Chang'er's fascination with the beauty routine did not amuse me. Since the day I gave her instructions on how to steam milk in the morning, she dragged her feet to get the pails ready while following me like a fly. What was she doing in the dark behind the pantry kitchen?

A few times I peeked through the window and found Chang'er staring at the milk in one of the pails while she stirred it listlessly with a metal spatula. Other times she struggled to lift each pail over the stove, snickering and mumbling to herself, then furiously swung her right forearm near the fire and over the pail of milk.

Once I could no longer suppress my curiosity. "My child!" I shouted. "You should stir milk with that long wooden ladle, not this rusty metal spatula. We aren't making an omelette!"

Chang'er froze, her one eye staring back at me, then burst into laughter. She flapped her arms and turned hysterical, guffawing. Even Old Yong rushed in to find out what happened.

"Hurry now!" I ordered her. "Stop fooling around like a monkey, you silly girl. Madame Chiang is waiting. See what happens if I report you!"

Keeping a straight face, I couldn't work out if I was more infuriated than tickled by her antics. It was in that moment that I first spotted the strange brown scar across her forearm—how she waltzed around, flinging her forearm, its sleeve rolled up to expose the unsightly flesh to the sun. All these years, the scar has lingered in my mind: it wasn't just hideous. It was a deformed horizon that had landed somehow on Chang'er's body. She sensed my curiosity. As if to block me from meddling and distract me from further questions, she leapt more energetically, threw her arm around me, and roared, "Isn't it lovely? Look at my impressive scar, Sister Green! No one in Shanghai can beat me at this beautiful work. A fortune-teller once told me, a woman with a prominent scar on one of her limbs was born not into wealth or luck, but blessed with courage and travels."

The week before Madame Chiang's forty-eighth birthday, I made plans for a banquet for eight.

"A modest dinner, Green," Madame Chiang specified. "Only Nancy, Dr. Kung, and their children will join the Generalissimo and me . . . Prepare some candies, some fruits for our nieces and nephews, but no birthday cake or candles. No creamy tarts, please."

I understood what she meant and decided to make some fried lotus roots with goji berries, mushrooms, and shrimps. With this main dish I proposed scallion oil noodles, pork and vegetable dumplings, water spinach with tomatoes, chilled tofu, and steamed egg. As for desserts, what could beat our traditional glutinous green rice dough filled with red bean paste, hardened egg yolk, and melon seeds? These were the comfort foods of a good family in Shanghai.

As we counted down the days, Madame Chiang, who was known to chide the Generalissimo for his long-windedness, reminded Old Yong and me repeatedly: "Just a plain Shanghainese family dinner." Our war against the Japanese had ended last summer, but the Rape of Nanjing had never ceased to haunt us. Eight years of fear, murder, and plague. Eight years of heartbreaks, disappearances, and numbness. The city smelled of death. Another war—this time against the Communists, the Eighth Route Army—was inevitable, though when, no one could tell. The Generalissimo, impervious to defeat, looked worn by the time he retired to bed. Nonetheless, he maintained his composure and routine: he slept by ten, rose at six. We looked out for Madame Chiang as best as we could. Old Yong went behind the Generalissimo's back and brought her more imported cigarettes.

No one dared to speak of the looming civil war, but it was hard to put on a stoic front day and night. Disquiet took its toll on the household. More and more uniformed guards entered the compound without informing us. They stood watch over us around the clock. One even came to the kitchen before every meal to verify that each dish had no poison. I became anxious by the day, keen to please Madame Chiang and to surprise her on her birthday. Who knew if there would be a next year, another banquet?

After dinner on the night before Madame Chiang's birthday, I told Old Yong that we were short of staff. I needed an extra pair of hands. Old Yong shook his head.

Without hesitation, Chang'er stood up from her seat and volunteered. "I'll come with you to the marketplace in the morning," she offered. "In time to return for my own work for the day." She winked at me.

The streets were throbbing with bustle and a cacophony of voices. Vendors squabbled among themselves at ad hoc stalls, selling herbs, spices, buns, fruits, and vegetables. Workers from the train station stood by the stalls, perspiring and wolfing down bowls of noodles with hot dumpling soup. In the crowd, a troupe of singsong girls distributed political tracts. They chanted patriotic songs. Carts and bicycles were stationed around trees and fences. The homeless slept on newspapers outside some clothing shops. Child beggars rambled along the sidewalks, which were lined with buckets of human feces and cartons of rubbish on abandoned pushcarts. Rickshaw pullers parked at the end of each pathway and hooted for passengers. In a compound under a sprawling plane tree, a clique of old women sat on creaky rattan chairs. They fanned themselves and gossiped without shame. Yet another new day had begun for the southern capital.

We scampered down one of the packed lanes before turning into the narrow street market, where Chang'er stopped short.

"What's wrong?" I could sense her enthusiasm peter out on the spot.

She turned around abruptly and stood before a torn wall, pasted with remnants of newspapers, handwritten announcements, and faded pictures. Her face ashen, she stiffened up and glared at a poster. It bore the portrait of a girl, sketched in black crayon.

"What does the poster say?" I elbowed her.

"An underground search warrant for an accomplice of the counterrevolutionaries."

"Who?"

Chang'er paused, transfixed by the poster. "A young peasant woman who helped her guerrilla husband flee the Communists. Apparently they were caught on the night of their escape."

"And?"

A rickshaw puller dashed past us, shouting in a dialect that we couldn't make out, and we swerved aside.

"The husband got away, but not his wife. She blinded one of her eyes with a fork and slashed her arm with a kitchen knife," Chang'er hastened to explain. "She fooled the militia with her bloody face and screams. They took her for a lunatic who lost her mind when her husband deserted her. She is still at large."

I gaped at the poster and dropped one of my empty baskets. I trembled a little, dumbfounded and unsure if I recognized the woman. Chang'er glanced at me, picked up the basket, and put her scarred arm around my waist. In a calm voice she coaxed me, as if no one else was in the streets. "Let's move along, Sister Green. Don't fret. Nothing will happen to us, trust me and do as I say. Just behave as if we'd seen nothing. No one will stop or question us.

We have a big day ahead of us. We have lots to buy for Madame Chiang's dinner."

Seventeen years have flown by, yet each hour crawls. Every story-teller knows when to omit the backstory, how to mend the foggy in-betweens. So when I do the same to my own account, having gotten used to replacing *I* by my full name, without the right to the honored *we*, I become my own protagonist, doomed to the mishaps of verity and the equally hurtful edges of fiction. Why did I dream of Chang'er last night? Am I polishing these scraps of memory for my confession? Long since have I given up hope for news from her—or from anyone of the Chiang household. No news portended good news: the girl couldn't have been safer than escorting Madame Chiang to New York and then Taiwan. I too would have tagged along had it not been for my aging aunt Lan, who could no longer walk because of her bound feet. My parents died when I was a teenager; Aunt Lan was my only kin. I could not live with the thought of leaving her behind to fend for herself in the streets.

Aunt Lan passed on in her sleep at age eighty-one, during the Great Leap Forward. It was a gentle death. No suffering, no knowl-edge of the end when it drew near. By then she had lost her hear-ing and memory, and I fulfilled my duty as a pious daughter. Every photograph, every keepsake in our possession that lingered from those Nationalist years, I have now burned or discarded without regrets. The white jade pendant cross was a gift from Madame Chiang on our last moon festival together. I had never worn it, not even before I stamped on it and crushed it as soundlessly as possible. Now I am one of the "capitalist roaders" who refuse to repent the old ways, a traitor who can't summon the courage to hurt myself the way Chang'er once did to pull through a calamity. But how savage—that the courage to hurt myself is the only way to save myself from persecution? Again, would I be slapped incessantly by armed student rebels during the next mass rally, humiliated and hauled down the street before an incensed mob in front of Madame Chiang's former residence, which was ransacked, vandalized beyond recognition even before this white terror? Who the heck was Old Yong? Did the rest of his family stay on in China? Did he collaborate with the Japanese? Why didn't he participate in the Revolution? Who was Chang'er? A friend or an enemy? Confess, confess.

Clenching a fork, I hold it up, close my eyes, and contemplate for the umpteenth time the odds of blinding an eye with the fork. Disfigure yourself, nags a voice in my head. I could plead for a lighter sentence. But times have changed, people's hearts emptied: who can be assured if that might not constitute an act of guilt, a show of cowardice, reinforcing in my accusers at the commune political committee their foul impressions of me—an incorrigible serf unable to confront her past, refusing to denounce the feudal masters whom she served, dead or alive?

Once a cook for Madame Chiang, forever a dossier and number. Now an old maid branded a revisionist spy, an unremorseful relic of the old aristocratic society—my name is Green, *qing*, as in the *luxuriant green*, the splendid nature. This is my real name. Complete in one word. One character. I have never been given a last or pet name. Not long after the Liberation, I published the recipe for Madame Chiang's *sela* in a popular women's lifestyle magazine based in Hangzhou. By any standards, it was scarcely elaborate: just a list of instructions based on what Chang'er told me, jotted down from memory. It wasn't a unique recipe. To appeal to a more contemporary woman readership—or so I was told—I invented some of the ingredients and measurements, emphasizing its nutrition facts, an iconic foreign taste. But I could neither write nor type. So I phoned the magazine office from a local district security bureau to dictate the recipe to an editorial assistant. A fresh graduate—her pen name was Typhoon—illustrated "my" recipe and spiced it up with a brief paragraph about my glittering past as the charismatic cook who ran Madame Chiang Kai-shek's household during the wartime forties.

Since I had adopted Chang'er's name, no one knew where I'd lived or worked. It goes without saying that I never got paid. Nor did I receive a copy of the monthly. Now that has sufficed as a long-standing evidence of my background history. Square characters, each the size of a window, were splashed in black paint across the brick walls of a two-story house opposite my detention center. *Never forget class struggle*, decrees the slogan. Instead of renouncing my dubious past and class status, I had blatantly reminisced about my old life, glorified it with nostalgia. I was hands down a capitalist roader. To the benighted masses of our New China, I promoted the private lifestyle of my former employer—one of the most condemned women in Chinese modern history, whose indoor shoes were tailor-made, embroidered with pearls once buried alongside the corpse of the imperial Dragon Empress Dowager Cixi, while the nation endured hunger, slavery, looting, and executions by the Japanese and Western colonialists.

Depending on my performance this afternoon, my degree of self-abnegation, I could be sent to a mental hospital in Shenyang or deported to Xinjiang for reeducation. Whatever they force onto me, I won't retaliate. I won't inflict violence on myself. I must make peace with the past with my thumbprint on every document presented to me. No doubt, no question, no opinion.

So let me come clean now, here, about my last transgression: Before our Great Proletariat Cultural Revolution broke out last month, I was still making *sela* for myself every weekend. I fixed myself the original version, the one concocted by Chang'er. Yes, the one she taught me when we first met. I ate it with a fork instead of chopsticks. I took my time to chew on it and smoked a Double Happiness cigarette after. I exhaled and savored dusk before our deputy chief warden put out the lights. I wondered how Old Yong was doing, if he was still alive. A radio crackled the evening news from my neighbor's room. Someone wept above—a woman or man, I couldn't tell. With or without sugar, the *sela* was too rich for me to finish in one meal.

A CHANGE OF WIND

1976

Comrades,
    I stole a recipe for a coded key. With straw and bamboo, I am unsure whether to make fans or mend sleeping mats. I have been reformed and fit a common rank. This is my second petition in six months. I would like to keep the sound of my name.

Qing 青—green.

Qing 清—limpid.

Qing 轻—light, lighter than a feather.

III

I kill an ant
and realize my three children
have been watching

KATŌ SHŪSON

THE INVISIBLE WINDOW

2016

Rows of empty pews grew longer. Like shadows, they straightened on their own before curving their tails. Three slim women trod single file down the side aisle, as softly as they could. A priest in a fern-green robe rushed across the bay with a plastic bag of oranges. He was headed for the arch door along the transept.

Ying slipped onto a pew and scooted sideways. Tong and Lou followed suit. Both tiptoed on their black and tan ballet flats. Ying hung by the edge of the pew with her feet off the ground. She was the only one in the church wearing heels. A few times, her faux leather handbag hit the pew in front of them. The clank of its metallic clasp against antique wood was the only intrusive sound in the cathedral.

Ying was annoyed, but pretended she heard nothing. She slid her way toward the nave. Like Lou, she wore a mid-length floral-printed dress with long sleeves and a discreet low cut. Their attire contrasted with Tong's somber look: a black collarless biker jacket over a black turtleneck with dressy black knit pants, and puffy eyes she could barely open but did not bother to hide with dark eyeglasses. The trio had short, breezy hair, chic enough to pass for models or actresses. They moved in tandem and signaled to one another more like sisters than old college friends.

A door in the back of the cathedral creaked open. Lou turned around. A visitor, perhaps, since the space was vacant on weekday mornings at the end of autumn. Like the eagle, one of the apocalyptic beasts in a stained-glass window at the entrance, silence flapped its wild wings.

The silence breathed but did not move.

Tong leaned over to whisper to us. "How surreal to meditate in Chinese here in Paris, in an ancient cathedral. We three musketeers took up fencing and majored in French and European studies . . . me and my foil, you two with épées. Almost thirty years ago. Would we have imagined ourselves here, who we are now?"

"Really, Tong, how do you meditate in Chinese? I don't think meditation exists in different languages," said Lou, though Ying could have easily said the same words.

"I don't think meditation exists in *any* language."

"Yes, I know. When we meditate, we aren't supposed to talk, let alone think in words. We're meant to invite the sacred into us, not let words lead us into a labyrinth of thoughts."

"Lou is right. Meditation means silence," said Ying.

"An emptiness that opens up to the unknown . . . the mystery . . ." said Lou.

"Saint Augustine calls it the interior life," said Tong, the French major. She went on to paraphrase her favorite saint: "'But you were within me when I was in the external world, and there I searched for you, rushing in my ugly state for your gracious creatures. You were with me, and I was not with you.'"

"I can't believe you can still quote from *The Confessions*!" said Lou.

"Memories come back—they always do. Weren't we studying the Western classics before classes were boycotted that spring?" said Tong.

"*Ma-ra-na-tha* . . . *Ma-ra-na-tha* . . . *Ma-ra-na-tha* . . . That is my mantra," said Ying. "It means 'Come, Lord' in Aramaic. Try it, both of you, and feel the difference in your bodies after twenty minutes or so. I meditate up to an hour. Just focus on gently repeating each syllable and breathe. As slowly as possible . . . take time to detach yourself from the present."

"*Ma-ra* what?"

"Easier said than done—"

"Your will is the problem. Don't put up a fight in your mind. Even the word lets go of itself when you finally release the voices in your head."

"So the word is an antidote for anxiety . . ."

"That instant you give up the past, the past gives up on you."

"Wow, no past or future—"

"Darling, you get more exotic each year."

"Drop it, Tong. I didn't come all the way here from Issy-les-Moulineaux to watch you girls bicker over—let's see, spirituality? Like it or not, we're stuck with one another for life."

"Meditation is just the worst form of yoga. No posture, no final resting pose. No corpse pose, Savasana, in which time slips away so we can wake up to yet another reality."

"Every year I remind myself to bring along a cushion, and I forgot it yet again!"

"You've until next year to remind yourself continually. Make that reminder a daily exercise—even better, a ritual. Mindful training constitutes great mental practice."

"Don't be pedantic. A yogi said, 'A cow is placid and doesn't need yoga or meditation.'"

"Where does your yogi come from? An audiobook this summer?"

"Do cows enjoy better karma than us humans? Cows are vegetarian, so they have a higher chance of reincarnation."

"Enough about cows. What are we supposed to do, sit still the entire time?"

"Nuns do. Monks too."

"Not me. I need to move my fingers on an invisible keyboard—"

"When I was meditating on my own, I heard voices in Chinese. Sometimes they approached me in echoes, as voices reverberating from the clouds. For a while, I thought our friends were talking to me while they floated as immortals somewhere up among the stars. Other times, their voices oscillated as waves. They dragged each word along the shoreline—"

"How incredibly lyrical. Tong, you're the poet who hasn't published a poem since we left Beijing. Look at you, eyes glued day and night to the computer screen . . . Don't waste time translating legal forms and affidavits for companies that underpay you. Write your sonnets and elegies. I'm relieved you said something about our friends. Last year, you broke down when I mentioned Ai, the cellist—"

"All right, Lou—stop reminding her of our faltering dreams. You know our grief will never leave us. Here is a term for our condition: post-traumatic stress disorder, PTSD."

"That's fine, I'm not offended. Lou is angry. Let her—"

"I disagree. We don't need therapy or religion."

"We aren't victims, we don't need pity or statistics."

"Nor self-help."

"I've never played victim. We are survivors."

"Yeah, right—we escaped the arrests and persecution during the crackdown, and here we are, *overseas Chinese*. We are the survivors who must carry on with the political work."

"Come on, I don't see how political our work and lives have become these days. We live in a capitalist society that granted us asylum. We were their refugees, and refugees mustn't make noise. Be grateful. Here money bears no odor and holds to no principle. Each for his or her own, the survival of the fittest."

"Freedom is an illusion without money."

"Oh yes, life is about business as usual."

"How naive we are—the diaspora of nostalgia who funds a revolution back home when the time arrives."

"Sometimes it arrives and knocks on the wrong door. Last month, a French radio station contacted me to ask me to comment on a bestselling title, a bande dessinée, a comic book about our movement—"

"A live interview?"

"How much did they offer?"

"We didn't reach the stage of negotiation."

"I doubt they pay. What did you say?"

"I said it wasn't just a movement. It was also a massacre. I told him I wasn't interested in fiction."

"How did the journalist take it?"

"He hung up."

"What comic book, a manga?"

"Who wrote the story? A Chinese?"

"How old was the journalist?"

"No idea. Thirties or early forties?"

"He wasn't even born when the massacre took place. What the hell does he know about June fourth?"

"Probably just the theoretical and media stuff he'd been taught to regurgitate. They're given a script to follow. They even verify facts based on the internet . . ."

"What? Since when is reality defined by what's shown or available online?"

"I try not to be skeptical from the outset, but honestly: these young Westerners don't know a damn thing about Zhao Ziyang or Hu Yaobang, not even Deng Xiaoping, let alone the reform policies and economic plans, the Chinese people's disenchantment . . . all the skepticism, the disillusionment that led to June fourth."

"Oh dear, did they imagine the June fourth carnage as some one-night battle?"

"Where did they get their information?"

"Social media?"

"More like imagination than information—"

"Those of his generation and profession know only what history textbooks and documentaries show. No real argument or new idea. To render their reportage more authentic, they would invite some front liners like us—"

"What do you mean?"

"Do they think what we went through that summer is merely rhetoric today? Have they even seen the Tank Man photo?"

"In any event, they seem curious enough to question facts or fiction. Unlike people back home, where amnesia has come into vogue . . . especially in our generation."

"June fourth is a folktale: selectively forgotten and forgiven when cash, comfort, technology are within reach—"

"This is pure academic dope. I bet there's a booming industry of dissertations, encouraged by prestigious university professors who weren't even at the crime scene."

"Yeah, intellectual vampires. A bunch of careerists and opportunists. Making a living off others' blood."

"Problem is, children listen to them. Students today are so obedient. They're pro-establishment. They follow hierarchies and navigate the mechanisms of power. I can't speak for students elsewhere, but look at most college kids in China. All they want is comfort, status, and success. The new middle class, no?"

"We lived by the instant; they strategize for their future."

"That's true. They don't even dream of going abroad anymore."

"So a novelist from London last year, doing research for her historical fiction. The year before, a Swedish broadcaster, and now a local radio station—"

"One day some screenwriter or film artist from New York will make a movie about the carnage. They'll call it an uprising. You'll see."

"Narratives with some sexy characters to drive a plot: conflict, climax, and resolution. Simple."

"Ah, sexy girls like us?"

"Why doesn't Ai Weiwei make a film about June fourth? He is out of China now. Someone told me he's moved to Berlin . . . Another said he might be moving again, this time to London or elsewhere . . . Drama, conflict, tension—"

"But no resolution."

"Didn't we have a Chinese writer win the Nobel Prize ten or fifteen years ago? He wrote a play about June fourth."

"You mean Gao Xingjian? His plays have been banned in China, haven't they? He lives here in Paris. Anyway, one play isn't enough. I've read it—in both Chinese and French. Too abstract for me, too elitist. That's the trouble with contemporary art. At some point, we need the mainstream audience to understand and *never forget*."

"What's wrong with being *abstract*? You make art sound like a public service—"

"Since you know so much about art, why not write something about it? Where is your poem about us?"

"Here she goes. *Why didn't you write something about it*, blah, blah, blah—"

"You know the truth. Write it."

"We've been through this, Lou. Leave Tong alone."

Again, silence—it breathed, but did not move.

Lou said, "Some of those pseudo-intellectuals denounced their own students to the soldiers the week leading up to our failed talks with Premier Li Peng. One by one, they switched sides and collaborated with the government. Now these hypocrites build their careers on rewriting history: reframing facts, inking out sources, manipulating narratives. Only two hundred students dead or missing?"

"They must imagine us fools," said Ying.

"That's the thing," said Tong. "People want to believe the falsehoods—that's how they survive. They've been brainwashed. No one on the mainland wants to recall the massacre anymore. Collective amnesia."

"My French neighbor still finds it absurd that the numbers 6 and 4 are routinely censored on WeChat and in emails. I told him, 'Try messaging someone in China with these digits together.'"

"It's time for us to make a trip to Hong Kong next year and join the annual vigil in Victoria Park. What have we been waiting for?"

"I agree. Hong Kong kids are different. They're our future."

"The Umbrella Movement was just the beginning—"

"Next year marks the twentieth anniversary of the handover. You read what happened in Mong Kok," said Lou, referring to the riots in February. "At some point, the Chinese will clamp down on Hong Kong too. The Communist Party stops at nothing."

"Those nerds may criticize the Chinese government, boast about their prodemocracy beliefs when they visit the West. But have the Westerners the slightest idea how these Chinese patriots behave once they return home for summer vacation?"

All three women knew only too well how these Chinese "patriots" bribed local university officials with invitations to overseas institutions.

"Conferences here, exchange programs and master classes there . . . *The Guardian* has reported that the Chinese have essentially bought Cambridge."

"Ha, a wolf in sheep's clothing."

"These scholars—politicians in disguise, deep inside they're cowards. They seek power or bow to it."

"When violence broke out, they did nothing but bawled. They watched it on TV."

"Since when are they the 'June fourth contemporaries'? Who invented these ideologies?"

"Librarians and archivists."

"So I gather. We're classified as assets for oral histories. All the more when we're fluent in English and French. Anyone can reach us by email now. The stained-glass window is broken, by the way. See?"

Tong pointed to a lancet window. Lou nudged Ying as the latter lowered herself to take off her high heels and rest her toes instead of paying attention to Tong.

"Just above the altar, behind the aluminum ladder and chairs. Weren't wooden planks protecting it last year? Why hasn't the cathedral done something about this since then?"

Plastered with irregular strips of makeshift glass, the medieval lancet window featured an armature with simple grids that generated a prism of red and yellow ocher with hypnotizing hues of violet and green. No one could know what was painted on the glass. The once-exalted images were gone. Poor angels and celestial creatures—they too had been in exile.

"I don't care for oral history or the broadcast present. I'm not going to betray our silence."

"Me too, our secrets follow us to our tombs."

"No one is obliging us to speak out. Does anyone even want us to? No one cares for testimonies when they speak from the heart. Despite the almighty internet, the public can't find the facts. Bureaucracies operate the same way everywhere, regardless of culture, language, or jurisdiction. Timeless and invisible, like silence, this annual memorial of ours."

"Who on earth meditates once a year for insight and mental well-being?"

"I agree with Lou. This reunion is no more than a symbolic act for lost souls who have no cemetery to go to, no place to honor their dead. It's our candlelight vigil for the massacre. I come because of my guilty conscience. Why are we alive instead of our comrades? If not for you both, I'd have given up on spiritual transcendence. Enlightenment isn't for me," said Tong.

Ying heaved a sigh. She looked up at the shattered stained-glass window. Pinholes of light twinkled on the ground, fickle yet nimble. They were competing for sluggish shards of shadows around them. The tiled space before the altar looked disrobed, and stones below the window unusually rugged. Tong checked her watch and nodded.

"It must be noon now. Look at that light. Subtle, isn't it? That energy seeping into the stones and walls . . . Hope."

"I'm hungry. All I had this morning was a hard-boiled egg. Let's go for risotto after, shall we? I know of this new Italian place near Châtelet. The chef is a Briton who married a former model from Naples—"

"Last year, you behaved like a pig. You ate and drank too much at lunch, and complained of stomachache barely ten minutes in. This is why this year we agreed to meditate first."

"Not to mention your farting . . . *Xiang pi bu chou, chou pi bu xiang*, loud farts do not smell, smelly farts aren't loud. How profound, this saying from home! When Grandpa taught me the line,

I had no idea how noble it was, that it was really about human deceits. Intellectuals who sweet-talk and fart versus—"

"Oh, shut up. We're in a place of worship."

"Hello? Doesn't freedom of speech apply in churches?"

"Can't you two stop arguing? Neither one of you has changed. Stop talking about food and farting. Concentrate on the luminous energy. If only this calm light could speak . . . What would it say to us humans when we're compelled to prayers, on our knees?"

"That depends on how well we listen?"

"And if we speak up—"

"Not just for ourselves . . ."

"Speaking of speaking up on behalf of the silenced . . . didn't one of our student leaders allude to the massacre as an apple on the tree, unripe but must fall to its fate at all costs?"

"He served a couple of years in the prison. Now free as a bird, a big-shot research fellow at an institute in America. His soapbox speeches have become quite sophisticated, or so I heard."

"He also traveled to Taipei to work on a book. It was about grassroots resistance in post-Mao China."

"I thought he was fundraising with wealthy businessmen who claimed to be prodemocracy. Still a bachelor, that suave scholar, smooth talker . . . I swear to God, if I bumped into him again, I would punch him in his face."

"Good thing you've kept your anger alive."

"We need to stay angry," said Ying, even though as an executive director at a life insurance firm in La Défense, she'd had to make peace with her ghosts to get through each day. "Consider meditation . . . the Christian notion of souls a great leap forward for me."

"Ghosts don't need to talk to me the way they do with you," said Tong. "They've never left me. In fact, I dreamed of Little Blue and Mogo a few nights ago. The same black-and-white dream that kept creeping up on me. Somewhere in the dream, I heard the guns and the screeching of brakes in a crescendo. I was hit by tear gas. But there they were, sitting on the floor, motionless as statues, meditating like us, except that they weren't doing it for themselves. They were protesting."

"Were they in the square?"

"Yes, in the middle of it, surrounded by chaos and flames."

"I don't call that place a square anymore. It was hell. Convoys of tanks rolling in and crushing our Goddess of Democracy into powder. Martial law troops called in to wipe us out. Lights turned off without warning. That eerie silence before the gunshots . . ."

"None of us was armed. Most of us asleep. Troops were shooting in all directions. Mortar round one. Mortar round two. Our metropolis of bloodshed."

The screams echoed in their head as they spoke of the crackdown.

"I was the one who had ditched Little Blue and Mogo in the tent," said Tong. "Yes, right there, before Team 629 brought us the last batch of Molotov cocktails. I'll never forgive myself for going home that night . . . I was planning to join them before dawn."

"We should have burned down the damned monument. Knock it down! Liberate the souls of the martyrs it commemorated! Remember how we paraded the Goddess of Democracy around the obelisk, blasting over loudspeakers Cui Jian's rock 'n' roll music? And our anthem, 'Heirs of the Dragon'?"

Ying hummed the popular Taiwanese song and Tong whispered the opening refrain:

In the far-off East flows a river called the Yangtze.
In the far-off East flows the Yellow River too.
I've never seen the beauty of the Yangtze
Though often have I sailed it in my dreams.

"Feels like yesterday . . ." said Lou, speaking for all three.

The masses of students sang in unison and chanted slogans on their bicycles down Chang'an Avenue. *Absolute power corrupts absolutely. To be or not to be.* They raised their fists and defied authority. Workers joined in soon after. They coordinated teams who took charge of water supplies and medical support. Some distributed pamphlets, wrote bulletins for the media.

"On some days, the whole protest site was an ocean of faces, a carnival—"

"A utopia."

Ying sniffled. Tong wiped her own tears with two fingers before they rolled down her powdered cheeks. She took over Ying's humming and added the lyrics:

It was a hundred years ago on a quiet night,
The deep dark night before the great changes,
A quiet night shattered by gunfire,
Enemies on all sides, the sword of the dictator.

"We held hands, crossed our arms and swung them, then packed ourselves into a jammed crowd. What a spectacle. We drank and sang in our hoarse voices 'L'Internationale'. . ."

Arise, ye starvelings from your slumbers,
Arise, ye criminals of want,
For reason in revolt now thunders,
And at last ends the age of cant.

"How off-key we must have been."

"We three vowed to sing it in French one day, remember?"

"Forget it, now that we live in France—"

"We became almost hysterical with joy when the Goddess of Democracy claimed her spot in the square . . . Were we naive to have imagined hope?"

"Lou took pictures . . . didn't you, Lou?"

"I had to destroy them before we left Beijing. But the negatives survived. I keep them in a storage unit near Gare de Lyon, together with your violin and old passport—"

"But wait," said Tong, still trying to describe her dream. "It was the night before our hunger strike. I saw Little Blue and Mogo in baggy green jeans and brown T-shirts with the map of America printed on the back. One moment they were sharing a cigarette and the next they were sleeping in their panties on soaked blankets and cardboards, beside a radio and bicycle, with buckets of red paint in a makeshift tent. Mogo wore her red headband and two green armbands, Little Blue her fake Gucci sunglasses. They smiled with eyes shut, oblivious to the mayhem around them. My, they looked like rock stars!"

"I bet that bachelor student leader saw what happened to them the night before the tanks rolled in. He didn't intervene . . ."

"Why would he? He left at gunpoint!"

"Where were you in the dream?"

"Rallying near them? I thought it was one of those peaceful nights. We were exhausted. Most of us who lingered couldn't find food."

By then the square reeked of garbage. Fires had erupted in the areas closer to the gate tower. Cars and bicycles were engulfed in smoke.

"I thought you were stationed in the southwest area, somewhere near the Great Hall of the People," said Lou.

"No, I wasn't in the dream," said Tong. "When I opened my eyes, I was nowhere but here, trying to meditate with both of you. I saw colors and silhouettes, then pairs of eyes staring at me. I found myself naked, like Little Blue and Mogo—"

"Those two idiots—they even yelled to me, 'Those are just blanks. They won't shoot us, don't be afraid.'"

"Remember how we found them dead? I know who raped them. That son of a bitch, he lusted after them during the demonstrations, sucking up to them, sticking around whenever he could go for it. He cornered them, zipping up and down his fly. I know where he is now. The bastard runs a taxi company and lives with his blind mother in Chaoyang District—"

"Listen to yourself. Have you done anything about him? If you want revenge, go ahead. You don't need our permission. For now, can't we just meditate?"

"We should count ourselves lucky to be alive: exiled to the same continent, so we could reunite after all these years."

"Yes, three old spinsters displaced in France."

"We haven't done too badly so far . . . If only justice—"

"Justice doesn't happen by default."

"There is no justice."

"At least we've stayed true to ourselves despite time and its wrinkles on our faces."

"The wrinkles belong to time, not us. So time is the haggard heroine. Not us."

"My dear beauty queens, I'm not a spinster. I'm twice divorced!"

"Well, Lou, as long as you're single, I regard you as a spinster like me."

"Aren't we part of a revolution? What difference does it make, married or single?"

"Right, *we* women hold up half the sky—that dictator said *women*, not wives."

"Yes, we women."

"For Little Blue and Mogo."

"Peace to their souls, and ours if we each have one."

"I don't want peace for my own soul. We don't have time to heal anger and all that crap. Lies spread like a virus, all thanks to the internet—from one language to another, country by country . . . Can you hear the sirens, smell the burnt corpses? Meditation can't stop ambulances dashing through the boulevard yards away."

"Be calm, yes, be angry—"

"We can never step foot on the square anymore . . ."

"All the exits were blocked."

"Because we lost."

"We died that night."

"We must live on—"

"Yes, because we are alive . . . because . . ."

A group of American tourists—two young couples in T-shirts and jeans, carrying lightweight travel backpacks and hiking staffs— approached the cracked stained glass from the right aisle in the nave. The girlfriends posed in the side chapel. A man squatted to capture more of the rounded vaults in the background of his photo. One of the girls hissed at him, and he turned around.

Like spectators seeing through the fourth wall, Ying, Tong, and Lou watched the visitors gesturing to one another like puppets in loud hushed voices. Ying frowned, then closed her eyes. Tong and Lou shrugged and surveyed the flying buttresses. Light filtered through the plasters. No one stood up to leave. They were not done with their meditation. Not yet. It must be past noon by now. The sun outside had tilted its face for a wider view. Piece by piece, light from the shattered window spread into a swath of yellow-blue. One of the American girls also began to study the flying buttresses. The young man bounced from his knees, brushed his shirt, and waved at Ying, Tong, and Lou. He nodded and pointed to his camera while his girlfriend and the other couple looked on eagerly. Why not a picture?

Tong and Lou hesitated before adjusting their bangs. The young American nodded again. He wasn't asking one of them to take a picture for him so he could join his friends. He was offering to take a picture of them on the pew. Ying opened her eyes. Quietly, Lou hid Ying's faux leather handbag behind Tong's back. What else to put aside to look relevant for a stranger? Three musketeers in a cathedral. The photograph would leave out their past thirty years and keep them intact at that moment—just before they finished their meditation. The women held hands and made sure to smile. They looked at one another instead of the camera.

IV

The winds that blow—
ask them, which leaf on the tree
will be next to go

NATSUME SŌSEKI

THE WHITE PIANO

1996

Before moving in, Willow had never known rue Séguier existed. She had quit her first teaching job in a lycée located across from the Luxembourg Gardens to try to become a pianist, but had found little work to speak of for her talent. She scraped out an existence in Paris and moved from one neighborhood to another. A year had limped by since Willow first transplanted herself from New York, after graduating with honors from Juilliard. No longer living off the largesse of her rich widow mother in Singapore, she took the new apartment with no second thoughts and despite its rent. After all, it was the only decent place she could have—without a laborious search or formal paperwork—where an upright piano was not considered a nuisance. For all she knew, most landlords, *propriétaires*—concierges, even—were more sympathetic to a dog or a cat.

When her friend Gaspard said that he had found her the perfect place in one of the best arrondissements in Paris, Willow mistook it for rue Suger. Also in the same neighborhood, the latter took its name from a medieval abbot and displayed on one of its ancient buildings a plaque that read: "On February 5, 1848, French writer J.-K. Huysmans was born here." Willow took a few days to pronounce the street name right: the *gui* should sound as a caustic *k* in French, brisk but exact, before it falls flat on a softer and more sensual *er*. After some practice before the mirror, Willow felt she could at last and with ease say it aloud in public. This was one of the things she must do to convince herself that she belonged to the address.

Séguier. She found out from a young assistant working at the *mairie*, the town hall at rue Bonaparte, that this was the family name of a French chancellor, Pierre Séguier. The Séguiers were members of one of the most powerful noble families, and Pierre lived during the reign of Louis XIV the Sun King. He would have seen Molière or Racine perform onstage—in tragedies and farces the dramatists wrote more for sustenance than for greatness. But what exactly did this Monsieur Séguier do? Willow's question must have seemed odd or persistent. The assistant's face turned from friendly to perplexed to irritated and stern. Caught between suspicion and ignorance, he picked up his desk phone and started talking to someone on the line, pretending that she was invisible.

The piano moved into the apartment a week before Willow did. But she had never acquired or rented a piano in Paris, she explained when the company phoned her late one night. She couldn't afford a piano, she said, trying to keep calm. And to tell the truth, she had planned to visit their showroom after settling in—to try out their secondhand pianos and look for a suitable instrument *by herself*.

In a croaky voice, the manager informed Willow that a piano addressed to her, sent by *someone in Asia*, was indeed waiting to be claimed. All that was required of her was a confirmed address, and they would be more than glad to make arrangements for the piano's transportation the next day. At reasonable costs, of course, the manager guaranteed. By then Willow had lost her patience, convinced that she was being swindled or pranked.

She slammed down the phone. It rang again. This time the manager assured Willow and spoke cordially, if not more prudently. He understood how confusing this must have sounded to her. Employees at this reputable piano company were just as dazed—and curious—when the instrument arrived unannounced at their storage unit in central Paris last week—all charges taken care of, on top of which a generous fee for their service in getting in touch with her the *propriétaire*, the owner. But this was no mistake or joke: a vintage white piano had arrived from Singapore. Willow, the manager reiterated, was not required to pay for it, but she had no choice but to accept it.

When Willow arrived at the hôtel particulier, the front gate opened by an automatic touch. A bleached white facade greeted her. Two cars and a bicycle were parked in the entrance court. Her studio apartment was on the second floor, in a separate building in the left wing. Still, moving a piano was a challenge. While the door seemed sufficient, the stairway was narrow and winding; the only way to move the piano was through the long French window from the entrance court-cum-parking lot. Moustafa, a professional piano mover contacted by the piano company, had proposed a fee of a thousand francs. Willow agreed. He arrived with his brother, the piano, and a few grimy mattresses and beddings in a vandalized pickup truck. Willow hid her surprise. She thought the piano would arrive solidly encased. This did not seem an auspicious start.

Although she couldn't yet get close to it, she saw from afar parts of its exposed top lid and music rack: they looked unwieldy despite the deceiving white. The rest of the piano was muffled up in layers of Styrofoam, Bubble Wrap, and torn carpets. After surveying the apartment from above and below, Moustafa walked up to Willow and said he needed ropes, cigarettes, and more men. He bent to tie his shoelaces, then asked for an extra four hundred francs.

The idea of seeing a white upright piano suspended by ropes and slanted in midair gave Willow vertigo on the spot. Four hundred francs weren't too much to ask. She agreed—it had to be done before the coming rain. But she made it clear that she would not pay more. Moustafa mumbled to his brother, who then waited with Willow in the entrance court. Both took turns smoking by the pickup truck until Moustafa returned with two muscular Algerians. By then it had started to drizzle, and everyone hurried to wrap up the piano with more layers of bedding until it looked like an oversize mummy with a fat belly. In fact, Willow told herself, it seemed like a pregnant woman, blindfolded and kidnapped and hauled up in broad daylight before going into labor or worse, suffering a miscarriage.

The two Algerians ran up to the apartment, pulled at the ropes, and shouted down. Moustafa and his brother gestured here and there under the dangling object. An old lady in the opposite wing of the building came out onto her balcony to supervise. Willow became jitterier by the moment. Something else pestered her too: despite its disguise, this piano felt familiar. This had more to do with its presence instead of appearance. Had she played on it before?

The piano, now resembling an ugly vessel, inched upward at what seemed like geologic speed. By the time it was inside, unpacked, and shouldered into a corner, it was pouring outside. In a rush, everyone left with the truck. Only Moustafa stayed. Willow was tired and did not sense anything amiss. Just as she was about to take her coat off and look for cash in its pockets, Moustafa threw her down onto the floor.

The wood floor was hard and cold against her back. She stared straight at the ceiling before realizing what was happening. Her heart throbbed. She knew what he was going to do next. She mustered her remaining strength and crawled for the door, crying out for help.

The loud rain poured, harder and faster. No one from the opposite wing could hear. Moustafa pounced on her again and dragged her toward him by her feet. He took out a rag from one of his pockets and stuck it into her mouth. From behind, he licked her left ear, dug one hand into her bra, and started rubbing her breast. She kicked, but she could not yell. She hit his chest with a fist, trying to break free. Moustafa roared, pulled her hair, and slapped her across the face.

Willow was overpowered, but she endured the pain and refused to weep. He kissed her with his tongue, while his other hand pulled down her skirt and underpants. There was no air, and Willow thought she was going to die.

But Moustafa's fingers found blood between her legs. The rest was a haze and a mess. He stormed out of the apartment, cursing in a mix of Arabic and French, and forgot to take the cash. Now the piano was dirty, disgusting, despite its white satin finish. The color out of place, the piano stood like a ghost. She wished for someone gentle to carry her to bed. Lying on the floor, she dozed off in the apartment—new and empty, save for the uninvited piano—until the rain stopped and she forced herself to gather her thoughts, put herself together, and go out for some hot food.

Most afternoons, Willow practiced. It was a Seiler, a German piano made during the First World War. At first she tried to find fault with its soft pedal and wondered if the piano might need tuning, but it worked just fine. After living with the instrument for a few days, she woke up one morning to realize that it *was* her piano after all. It was the piano she had played as a child. The piano her mother had played until a miscarriage, before Willow.

Her mother was a successful cook who emigrated to Singapore from Taiwan in the seventies. Willow knew little about her mother's past, except that she started as a maid for Madame Chiang Kai-shek during the war. She also married young, to a Nationalist sympathizer who infiltrated local guerrillas and never returned. In Singapore, she worked at the five-star Shangri-La Hotel until her remarriage. Her Singaporean husband—Willow's father—owned Chang'er, a fine dim sum restaurant chain named after her. He gave her a comfortable life. At home, she taught herself English and French and learned piano from a British professor. When she played with her calloused hands, she hid the scar on her right arm with long sleeves. She told everyone that her scar was a kitchen accident when she was little. Music consoled her during her grief and pregnancy. She had Willow in her mid-forties. The piano was a womb that had protected both mother and daughter, except one of them stopped playing once the other showed talent.

Willow phoned her mother, but no one answered. In a frenzy, she scribbled a letter to thank her for sending the piano, even if she wasn't sure of her own gratitude or the piano's dubious meaning. She hoped for a response, but her mother never phoned. Instead, she wrote back swiftly—a week later—to ask if Willow needed money.

Not at the moment, Willow wrote back. She was disappointed by her mother's taciturnity, but took it as her way to discipline her. To make herself feel more at home, she started giving private lessons and working on her audition repertoire: Bach, Brahms, Chopin, Mendelssohn, and from time to time, Hindemith or Prokofiev. She seldom began each piece from its beginning and kept the best for the last hour of her daily practice.

The old lady in the opposite wing looked out her balcony dispassionately each time Willow played Brahms. Sometimes the lady smoked or had a wineglass in her hand. She was visibly ill and often distraught. She idled on the balcony in her silk pajamas, her hair tied in a bun—inexplicably, she reminded Willow of Proust, except that she had no moustache—and wore a sad, vulnerable look. She was so still and fragile, like a vase that might be blown off the balcony by a gust of wind. Nodding to Willow with a thin smile, the emaciated old lady would mouth some words, and Willow would greet her with a soundless *bonjour*. Then the woman would turn her back as if there were someone else talking to her from inside.

At first whenever Willow saw the haggard old lady, Moustafa—really, who was this bastard, and where did he come from?—crossed her mind until she recognized her ruminations made no sense. Later that summer, Willow started to work, note by note, on a complete suite of intermezzos by Brahms. But by fall, the old lady no longer looked out her balcony. The windows were shut.

Where rue Séguier began, there was a rare books and antique manuscripts shop—gothically designed with boutique signs painted bright maroon and blue—which never opened for business except for appointments. The clientele was exclusive—for the *riche* and the *célèbre*—and only upon invitation. President François Mitterrand, Monsieur Le Cordier her *propriétaire* mentioned offhandedly, bought his first-edition books from this shop. In no way *riche* or *célèbre*, Willow, however, was expected for a rendezvous, an appointment on the first of each month, outside the bookshop. "This is where you give me your rent," Monsieur Le Cordier said to her. It was the only time he ever spoke to her in English.

Monsieur Le Cordier was a tall, lanky Frenchman who combed his white hair backward on both sides behind his ears and never failed to wear a suit on every occasion. Each time he wanted to say something important, he looked down from his glasses and raised his eyebrows. Polite but guarded, he spoke softly, formally, in articulate and elegant French. Never had he laughed or reacted when each month Willow gave him the cash: three or four rolls of fifty- and hundred-franc notes fastened with red elastic bands, and pieces of twenty-franc coins taped together, each stack for a sum of a hundred francs, and a total of a hundred in stacks of coins that added up to a thousand francs. *C'est parfait*, he would say. The talk between them hardly ventured beyond the general, either about the weather or her piano: *Je préfère Bach à Brahms*, he confirmed.

Someone else too was listening to Willow. It was mid-July, one of those suffocating summer days that make it impossible to stay indoors. She was sure everyone else was away for vacation; no car was parked in the entrance court. She pulled back the curtains and left the windows wide open. Again, she played Brahms's Intermezzo in A major. Her fingers got stuck at a familiar passage, where she kept missing the semiquavers because of the soft pedal, so she replayed it. Out of the blue, a head popped out of a window on the top floor that usually remained shuttered. It was the retired architect Monsieur Fournier. He waved, and since their windows were so close, he didn't even need to shout: "Come up, mademoiselle. I want to show you my piano."

The lofted space, its Baroque chandeliers and sparkling wooden floors, took her breath away. Behind him, a Pekingese stuck out its tongue and wagged its tail. Monsieur Fournier gestured to her to follow him into another room, and as she followed, Willow stole a glimpse of the rest of the place—the space of a whole-floor apartment—before sitting at a Bechstein concert piano. The touch was impeccable. She could smell the perfume of each note and feel the shape of it as if it were a pearl. Were she able to perform Debussy, she would have shown off a prelude or two right away.

As Willow started playing the Brahms Intermezzo, Monsieur Fournier smiled—in a sly way—as if he'd known that it was all she could play. When she was done, he told her that she could play on it anytime she wished, as long as the maid was around to open the door for her.

So began a new routine. Instead of working on her upright piano in the afternoon, Willow made her way to Monsieur Fournier's apartment, heavily furnished in a nineteenth-century decor with glazed doors and mirrors—Monsieur Fournier was virtually always absent—and when she had enough of rehearsing, she could peek into the other rooms, unseen by the maid. One day she felt bold and at ease enough with a space not hers to transgress a little. Instead of staying in the piano room and the right wing of the apartment, she walked across the high-ceilinged salon, the salle à manger, the study, the *chambres*, bedrooms . . . all the way to the luminous kitchen. The maid was there, ironing. As if she felt intruded upon, she stared at Willow with a surly expression. Unsure what to do next, Willow asked the maid for a glass of water.

"*Sur la table derrière vous,*" muttered the maid. *On the table behind you.* The maid returned to her ironing; Willow would not be served. The Filipina pounded her iron on the board and ran it across a long garment before slamming it down on the side, only to repeat the procedure on another fabric. It was hard for Willow to dispel the qualm that were she neither a woman nor an Asian, the Filipina maid might not give her such a cold shoulder, let alone resent her. It did not help that Willow looked young even for her age and presented herself as an artist, her hands manicured. The maid's distaste was as transparent as steam from the electric iron, which managed to work without a thermostat.

That night, Monsieur Fournier phoned—Willow thought he sounded far away . . . was he calling from China or his kitchen?— and without mincing words, he stated that he was disappointed to learn of her recent behavior in his home because the maid had told him that . . .

The mention of the maid insulted Willow. She dashed to the window with the phone in one hand, and yelled that yes, she took a sandwich with her for a rehearsal and so what, but no, she didn't invite a man into his apartment! No, she did not help herself to the apartment as if it were hers! No, she did not sleep in one of his beds. Yes, she asked the maid for a glass of water, and guess what! The maid said no! The maid is a liar! And he was a senile prick who believes liars! Infuriated and hurt, Willow slammed down the phone without giving Monsieur Fournier a chance to respond and shut the windows with a violent bang.

She never went back to Monsieur Fournier's apartment again, in spite of the written apology she received from him via the concierge a week after. The Filipina maid continued her cleaning rounds on Thursday mornings. From her windows Willow could see her arrive, cross the entrance court, open the door to the building, and walk up the lavish marble stairs to the top floor. Bitter and vindictive, Willow would stand at the windows, making sure the maid could, from afar, see her or feel her presence. She despised the maid, whose clothes smelled of their laundry detergent. Apparently the maid had been fired by the madame who owned the entire *rez-de-chaussée*—the ground floor—before Monsieur Fournier took pity on her. *That* madame was the wealthiest of all in this hôtel particulier, said her friend Gaspard, who until then had disappeared from the radar since Willow moved in. She was well over ninety and the widow of Schlumberger, the French oil industrialist and tycoon. Her son, a film producer, worked in a small annex behind the right wing, next to the hidden verdant garden.

It all made sense to Willow: without bothering to put on her slippers, she had come down one evening to take her trash to the recycling bin. There she bumped into a short and disheveled figure who looked uncannily familiar. Certain that he was none other than Al Pacino, Willow froze—no, she couldn't believe hearing herself ask in a meek, halting English, "Are you the Godfather?" To which the man glared back stiffly and answered in a raspy voice, "No, and whoever you are, I have had enough of your Bach prelude."

After several phone conversations that lasted late into the night, Gaspard confessed. Willow wanted to know how he managed to have come across this apartment. Everyone in the hôtel particulier was related to one another in some way. Much as no one ever bumped into someone else, if not for soirees or funeral receptions, and in spite of this, the walls had eyes and ears, there was no way an outsider could rent a place that belonged to this closed world. One of the families, she'd learned, had owned the entire second floor since the war of Napoleon.

"Your studio used to be my part-time apartment," Gaspard admitted with a soft sigh. "I needed a place to see my mistress. She was a student at the Sorbonne. She came from Shanghai, by the way. Where better than a studio in the Latin Quarter? When the affair was over, I went back to my wife, to my full-time apartment . . . How about lunch at Café Marly this weekend? We can talk more. Anyway, I want to know how you're doing."

Gaspard did not show up. Willow wanted to see him, not to catch up about the affair that was over, but to blurt out that her savings had run out and that she was planning to move out of rue Séguier. Since she would expect Monsieur Le Cordier to retain her six-week deposit, she had no intention to pay the last month of rent. Naturally, she ought to inform Gaspard, her rent guarantor and the go-between.

But the truth was something else: Willow couldn't imagine herself making love with anyone where she was living. Her piano—not the bed, a slide-away sofa bed—took up too much space in that apartment, which turned out to be more suffocating and sinister than her alcove studio back in Morningside Heights.

Feeling let down by the futile wait, Willow ordered a spiced orange salad with mint and vanilla and lingered at the café. From the arcades of the Louvre, where she sat, the view was crisp and beautiful. On a whim, she decided to seek out the gallery of Baroque paintings, and, in particular, something that had been on her mind for months.

According to the caption, the "monumental equestrian portrait" of Chancellor Pierre Séguier was painted by his protégé, Charles Le Brun, whose legacy was eternalized by his architectural decor genius of Château de Vaux-le-Vicomte, the Louvre, and Versailles. The painting itself, she read, had a turbulent history: confiscated at the end of the French Revolution, it had hung in the city hall of Troyes until reclaimed by the descendants. Later one of them—a baroness—kept it in hiding until her death in 1938. Willow was puzzled: why turbulent? Confiscated, yes, though being reclaimed by the descendants and then kept hidden seemed quite reasonable. What was hidden to one was safe to another.

Willow inspected Pierre Séguier up close. He stared straight into her eyes, but she couldn't tell from the oil painting if she liked Chancellor Séguier, or even liked the look of him. He was trim, with thick eyebrows and a moustache, and he wore a long robe of imperial yellow. One part of her thought he appeared pompous; the other part saw it as the grandeur of, as the caption stated, "neither a warrior nor a conquering hero" but of an "enlightened" patron and statesman. Who knew if women of that *époque* had seriously considered such a man young and handsome—he simply manifested social status. The year was 1660. Shown on horseback with six pages at his feet, Pierre Séguier was parading at the entry of Louis XIV into Paris—a theatrical mise-en-scène of a dignified person in "measured harmony and interplay of posture, reminiscent of the ballet." Right in the center of the portrait, the chancellor appeared to smile but with reticence. Was it seduction or pretense?

Observing her proximity to the painting and the way she scrutinized it, a group of Japanese tourists began to bustle in Willow's direction, cameras at the ready. She turned around and couldn't help but laugh. "Do you know why I'm looking at this portrait?"

Willow asked the visitors. A woman with a white Chanel bag shook her head.

"I live at a hôtel particulier at rue Séguier, and this distinguished man is Monsieur Pierre Séguier," said Willow. "I've a stingy land-lord called Le Cordier, who lives on the first floor. And a paranoid neighbor, Monsieur Fournier, on the top floor. They have grand pianos, but they don't know how to play. Monsieur Fournier sleep-walks in the entrance court. He needs Monsieur Le Cordier to put him back to bed. What's wrong with these wealthy old men?"

The Japanese tourists widened their eyes, unsure whether to laugh or to comment. Willow was pleased with her rumors. A man asked, "Where are you from?"

She paused, then cleared her throat. "I've been in Paris for a year. I wanted to move back to New York. But I've changed my mind. I'll buy a dog and call it Séguier."

When Willow wrote home—this time to accept her mother's help with the rent—she tried to describe the place in a way that might intrigue her stoic mother: Old and discreet, rue Séguier runs between rue Saint-André-des-Arts and the Quai des Grands-Augustins. The sun does not enter except in high summer and in random shafts, so the street lives in its shadow and protects its own peace. It is tangential to the Seine, sandwiched between two busy streets where tourists eagerly buy postcards, snap pictures of Notre-Dame, and order paninis from fake crêperies. I wonder why few visitors are reluctant to make a turn and venture down this path. Were the illusion of a mere residential street too perfect to be true, its sense of austerity would have shunned the foreigners. Behind closed doors and damask curtains, life carries on much as in a novel without a proper end. Bells from the favorite cathedral of Paris echo in the midst of Bach or Brahms. Up in the air— a piano is safe wherever it lands.

READING A TABLE

1976/1996

Since Cloud was a child, she had been fascinated with tables. Her grandfather, a self-taught carpenter from Shanghai who chose exile in Hong Kong before the Communist takeover, then went to Singapore, where he built a modest reputation during the sixties and seventies—first for restoring antique tables for galleries and museums, later tailor-making tables for luminaries and obscure figures alike. Grandpa's workshop, behind his shophouse at Joo Chiat Road, was open for business every day from twelve to midnight. Bulky handsaws, logs, and beams leaned against the brick walls. Lying in stacks were rugged boards, rods, and sawn timber between milling machines, in a maze of pipes, carts, tools, and cartons.

In this dim workspace down the narrow aisle, Cloud shook hands with a former state minister as her grandfather introduced her as his monkey disciple. There was also a stocky gangster from Chiang Mai who ran a casino and kept three mistresses in Indonesia. He wanted his name carved into the top of a rustic red maple table, to be styled in the most intricate calligraphy of his choice. "Make it look like the naked fairy tattoo on my chest," the mobster hollered, and took off his shirt, grinning. The request was flatly turned down: Grandpa told him in plain words that the picture in his tattoo was as vulgar as the act of engraving and etching it onto a table. Manual work must be respected, Grandpa emphasized, flaunting a drawknife before the bewildered gangster.

In Grandpa's private workspace, Cloud came to believe glories were made with hands, as she grew up with more unfinished tables and unsanded surfaces than ready-made tables and polished workpieces. Tables, in her mind, usually had three legs—leaning on either side, waiting to be upright.

Grandpa never saw in a table an object without a life. Round or oblong, he used to say, a table embodied a world: we sit at a table to find company. A table for a reunion, he added with pleasure. Interested in tables of all kinds—altar tables, meal tables, night tables, writing tables, folding tables, even ones for chess and table tennis—he read a table not just by the structure of the source trunk, the nature of its wood, the wood's place of origin, the table's overall appearance and function. He judged it by some measure of character or emotion: Would the table be happy in this human world? Or had its height, its asymmetrical form made it too rebellious to adapt to the new environment?

"Who are its ancestors?" Grandpa asked a sous-chef aloud when he came across a rare mahogany table in a Chinese restaurant at a lavish hotel near Orchard Road. Guests at the other tables heard Grandpa's strange question. They looked up. Ignoring the commotion, Grandpa ordered the signature starter, Madame Chiang Kai-shek's salad, followed by beggar chicken in clay and lotus leaves, an imperial dish from Hangzhou, and carried on, asking, "The earth or its trees or its emperors?"

A table was sacred because it kept a soul alive. "Carpenters don't build 'things,'" he told Cloud one night, after failing to repair a table infested with beetles. "We carpenters construct with wood an inner life that exists in a form to serve others." Once a table was built and done, it must stay. Not just for long, but for a generation, and others to come.

The table in the heated kitchen was the spine of their house, the wooden square where three generations had shared their meals together. A weathered ginkgo table with a drawer, which seated four—but they had managed to squeeze eight there throughout the years. Grandpa built the table in the sixties, without the need for a nail or screw. How was it possible? Cloud couldn't believe her eyes: grooves were locked into one another with traditional joins made out of enchanting geometric patterns. At the table they ate, laughed, and blabbered together. There, they went through bitter quarrels and patched up, however reluctantly, when ginger fish soup was placed in the center.

After dinner, Grandpa counted money at the table. Then he laid out a panoply of brushes, seals, and rice papers, grinding an inkstick on the family inkstone. His best brushes, dating back from the Meiji and Taishō eras, were from Japan, where like most progressive intellectuals and artists of his generation, Grandpa had studied. Grandpa wrote letters and petitions. Every so often he inserted cash in the envelopes. In ancient Chinese, a table was called *an*—in other words, a file, a case, a dossier.

"Yeye, why does a table have four legs, not three?"

"Because you're talking about a square or rectangle . . . If a table is small and round, it doesn't need more than two legs. Two legs or four limbs . . . like us humans."

"How about six? Can a table have six legs? Or four legs and two hands?"

"No, darling. Six is a divine number. It means a smooth life, a perfect path. Nineteen sixty-six, 1976, 1986 . . . any year ending with 6 is a round year. In Chinese divination, we mortals aren't supposed to lead a life too perfect to be true."

"Yeye, can a table be round and evil? What should we do if we sit at an evil table?"

Silence.

"Yeye, can we talk to tables?"

"Of course, dear. Tables have stories to tell us. Sometimes they tell us what we don't want to hear. You must learn to read them."

"Read stories or tables?"

"Both. Tables aren't any different from books—they have faces. Tables are open books. They don't need words."

"What happens when we talk to tables? Do they talk back to us?"

"Only if you listen."

"How?"

"Never knock on the surface and treat a table as a door."

"Yeye, do tables die? What happens when they die?"

Grandpa leaned forward to shift the plate of stewed peanuts closer to Cloud. They bowed and gulped their dinner in silence. When their gazes met, Cloud giggled and Grandpa smiled. This was one of the few quiet meals, only the two of them in the house. It felt like a ritual. Cloud came home early from school, so they dined early—at five. Grandpa cooked brown rice and a generous plate of stewed peanuts in soy sauce, alongside two small dishes of steamed tofu, mixed with strips of spicy Japanese zasai, pickled vegetables. There was no soup in the center.

"Yeye, why can't I fall asleep at a table?"

"Because that brings bad luck. You'll have dreams that are not yours, but of those who've sat at that table. You might even sleep-walk and never wake up."

"Why can't I sit at the corner of a table?"

"A corner is sharp. It cuts—like a dagger. In four directions: north, south, east, and west. An evil spirit intrudes from the corner . . . it enjoys looking over one's shoulders. That's how the spirit invades a family, our community, or whoever."

"What should we do with ghosts at a table?"

"My dear, most of them are harmless. They haven't yet passed to the other world. Meanwhile, they find kind families to take them in for a meal or two."

"Yeye, what should we do with Cousin Crystal's ghost at our table every dinner?"

Silence.

*

Cloud folded the wrinkled picture and discreetly slotted it underneath the table. At each meal, her fingers reached for the picture and tinkered with its ragged edges. It was a photo in sepia, its light too exposed, the image blurred. Cloud was the chubby girl in the picture, sitting on bulging white cloth diapers on a wooden bed that possessed no legs. She was four—maybe five—and bald, with a few streaks of hair. The bed came in the design of a huge wooden crate: rectangular, at ankle height, with eight wheels. There were horizontal beams on each side as supports, to protect Cloud from falling off her crate bed—a wooden vessel that skittered across the floor like a giant spider. It was an oversize toy from Grandpa, made specially for his granddaughters. Inside the crate bed were thin mattresses and handmade quilts with kaleidoscopic images of fish, nightingales, peacocks, elephants, bears, lions, dragonflies, and pandas . . . Cloud was playing with a box of wood building blocks and her pink wooden toy piano. She looked up at the camera with her mouth open.

A shadow lurked in the bottom left corner. It was her cousin Crystal, who took the picture. The girl seemed happy too, and was nine at that time—her hair, long to the waist and plaited. Cloud envied her older cousin's beautiful hair. She wove a flower—a delicate white orchid—into Crystal's hair, waved a wooden handheld mirror at her before running away. The photo was taken with Cousin Crystal's green instant Kodak camera, just as they began their hide-and-seek in Grandpa's workspace.

Crystal ran to a dusty corner behind the milling machines and old sawn boards. She hid under one of the half-finished tables. The crude pine tabletop, seven by nine feet, was stringed to four fluted legs. Bricks and slabs were laid on it to test its endurance and weight. Grandpa wasn't done sanding and lacquering the surface. When the table crashed, no one but Cloud heard it. A saw dropped, followed by several lathe chisels. Nails and blood all over.

"Where did these nails and chisels come from? What were you two doing in the dark? My god, what should I tell my sister?" Cloud's mother fired the questions at her daughter and wailed. In a rage, she slapped Cloud twice across her face before Grandpa stepped in. An ambulance arrived. Cloud did not tell her mother everything. For two weeks the girl said nothing. But it was not until Grandpa burned the broken table—along with every piece of wood, saw, and tool that had to do with this curse—out in the quadrangle when everyone, including little Cloud, accepted that a life was over, never to be mentioned again.

—*Wake up, my child. Don't fall asleep at the table.*

—*What happened? Has the joss stick burned to its end? Where am I? Is this a dream?*

—*You're safe, darling. Don't worry. No one is around. Don't cry anymore. Your eyes are all swollen.*

—*Cousin Crystal, is that you?*

—*Yes, dear. I'm here.*

—*I'm tired, but I can't sleep. It's been so long since my thoughts stopped racing. How I wish I could have a good night's sleep.*

—*You're not alone, my child. I've always been by your side. What're you doing on the balcony, kneeling before the altar table? It's past midnight. You must be shivering in this cold. Out there is a moon-glazed street staying up for the last traveler.*

—I'm praying to you, Cousin Crystal. I feel lonely. No one talks to me. Can you hear me when I call for you?

—Of course, my dear. Yeye hears you too.

—Yeye? Where is he?

—Right here, by my side. He can't talk to you, but we're watching over you.

—Yeye, I've so much to tell you! I miss Yeye, Cousin Crystal . . . he's been gone so many years. Has he been all right?

—Yeye is fine. He's never left you, little Cloud. He thinks of you every day. He wants you to know that he's proud of you. Look how time flies—you've grown into a lovely young woman. Soon you'll move to New York and start life afresh. Imagine the future, how exciting. An ocean stretches beyond its first light. We see love and contentment ahead of you.

—It's so misty, I can't see what lies ahead of me . . . I can't let go of the moon.

—You must, Cloud. One day you'll let go of us.

—I'm afraid of forgetting you and Yeye.

—No, you won't. Be confident, my love—go where brightness holds out for you. Don't get used to being alone.

—Cousin Crystal, is Yeye still making tables?

—No, my child. Not anymore.

—What does he do now?

—He comes home every night to the kitchen. Can you feel his presence? He's reading the Evening Post *at our meal table. Sometimes he practices cursive calligraphy. Sometimes he listens to music and writes to his friend Old Dan in Shanghai. Yeye talks about his apartment at the Wukang Mansion in its heyday. Last night, he made us shrimp*

and bok choy steamed dumplings. He's happy sitting there, looking over your shoulders. Watching over you.

A medium approached Cloud at the Westside Market on her way home one afternoon. Cloud was tired from a rough day at work, on top of her insomnia, but wanted to drop by the supermarket before hopping on the No. 1 downtown train.

"I'm Crystal," the African American woman said. "I work for the spirits."

Cloud stopped short and shuffled the groceries in her hands. She tried a wiry smile. Had she heard the stranger correctly?

The woman glared at her. She had a glass eye on the right. Her hair was tousled, as if she had been running, and came with a fringe that flashed streaks of purple and dark red. Her outfit was chic: a blue blazer and a low-cut gray blouse with white pants. She wore an eccentric dragon-head bangle around her right wrist. A large silver-plated lotus flower locket hung between her breasts.

She caught Cloud by her left arm, and Cloud flinched—she could feel the stranger's fingernails and her refusal to budge.

"Sorry, I don't know who you are," Cloud said. "What do you want?" she asked brusquely.

"I've a message for you, dear. Are you familiar with table-turning?"

Cloud shook her head and looked away.

"You'll know why I talk to you once you see my sacred place in Harlem," said the medium. "Come, follow me?"

"No." Cloud panicked. It must be a scam. She collected her thoughts and turned, hoping to escape.

But the supermarket was thronged. The customer behind her was impatient. He helped himself to a checkout divider and stuffed his items onto the conveyor belt. A security guard at the exit must have sensed something amiss. He threw a watchful glance in their direction. Cloud wanted to drop everything and run. She wanted to duck into the subway station right outside.

"I don't want your money," the medium insisted. "I must help a lost soul who needs to pass you a message before moving on. Why don't you give it a try?"

Hurriedly she reached out to help Cloud with the bags and shambled off in another direction. She limped a little, panting. A few times she turned around to check if Cloud was following.

Cloud gave in. She dragged her feet, thinking for a minute that the woman spoke with a distinct Shanghainese accent. In fact, she thought, the spirit medium had spoken to her in Shanghainese.

And that was the first thing Cloud told the investigators when she was summoned to the 28th Precinct police station in Harlem the next morning. She was not suspected of wrongdoing, not to worry, but did she recall anyone loitering around or inside the building?

No, Cloud responded. She agreed to cooperate with the interrogation. A spirit medium invited her into a shady red room on the top story, that was true. Was she a fraud? That wasn't up to her to judge, Cloud said. The woman did not ask for money. She seemed to live and work alone. The room wasn't locked when they arrived. It probably never was.

No, the medium didn't even ask for Cloud's name. Cranky,

wasn't it? She served coffee and fresh shortbread from the Westside Market. Their session began. What session? The table-turning. The investigators sniggered before keeping their faces straight. What did they do during the table-turning? Cloud placed both hands on the table and closed her eyes, listening to what the medium had to say.

The building was derelict, yes? Did it smell of a gas leak? Not quite, although the windows were shut with thick red drapes and Cloud found the room suffocating, the space gloomy and filled with smoke. Papers, clothes, and empty liquor bottles were scattered over the floor. Candles and joss sticks burned on a round wooden table and the stools around it. The wobbly table was marred by random scrawlings and sketches. Did she mean graffiti? More like solicited threads of thoughts and visions, she preferred to say. There were no chairs, however, so they sat on the floor. There were empty picture frames, strange religious figurines, and broken wineglasses on the table. Wasn't she frightened? Or nervous? Not really . . . well, not at the time of the séance. She was curious, rather, intrigued, and wanted to get to the bottom of the story.

What story? The medium claimed to have a message for Cloud from someone close to her. Someone from her childhood, she explained. What message? The medium went into a trance very quickly. She stood up and practiced automatic writing on the table. She scribbled four Chinese characters, *xi yi bu ce*: it cannot be understood by seeing or hearing. Wait a minute. Did the African American medium write and communicate with Cloud *in Chinese*? Sir, she did. What else did she say? What did her Chinese phrase mean?

That it couldn't be understood by seeing or hearing—this was the literal translation. Did Cloud understand the cryptic message? Who did it come from? Why didn't she ask any questions?

The spirit medium said the truth would dawn on Cloud sooner or later. She told her not to throw away her late yeye's green rotary phone. She also advised her to inform her family about the man she was seeing. Why? Did he do something wrong? Or was it because he was a white and European? The trance lasted around fifteen minutes. The table tilted toward Cloud before its candles were blown out abruptly by a cold gust. No, it did not levitate. Were the candles and joss sticks the cause of the fire? Any casualties? What about the medium—was she safe? It was Cloud's turn to ask questions. She would not tell the police everything.

The fire was still under investigation, an officer confirmed, but so far no evidence suggested arson. The entire top story was reduced to ashes. Luckily, no one was found dead. The spirit medium whom Cloud took pains to describe in detail was nowhere to be found.

Cloud wanted a table for her wedding.

"Just a table," she told her fiancé Yves after she was home from the precinct station in Harlem. Yves raised his eyebrows.

But no, his bride-to-be wasn't joking. Nor was she making some erratic mental list. The table should be made of light oak or walnut. She wouldn't mind cracks and wormholes, she added gently. A small table, but with slender limbs. Enough for a vintage phone, an empty notebook, and their vase to hold a lasting branch of ghost orchids.

NEITHER AN ELEGY NOR A DREAM

1996

Yeye caught a tiger in a stone and carved a stone into a tiger. He wasn't angry with the power the stone and tiger had wielded. In time he built bridges, boats, and cupboards. After a coma, he left us a foundation in his name to run. The bed he made for me surrendered its shape when I suspended the moon in my body. Now and then I asked the door if he'd return with the clothes he died in. His noble face, too discreet to weep. The shaman believed I betrayed my clairvoyance. Quick, swallow all the coins you have stolen. The dead always punish odd spirits. Even a cloud diviner needs a crystal. Two passwords: crystal and cloud. In my sleep, a vulture was arranging its feathers at my feet. I fidgeted but held my laughter. Premonition ended like a fruit fallen. In defeat, in plain colors. My grandfather initiated our pact. No time to fall ill, no time to heal. I wasn't young, but I was forgiven. I took the same road, braved the same sun. I rode on shadows and looked for white. Trying to memorize our last time.

BACK TO BEIJING

2016

May 6, 2016

Dear Su,

A surprise bouquet has arrived—how exquisite, these lilies—but what should I do with them? Did you send the gift? I counted, thirty-six lilies! Michel is allergic to pollen, though. He joked that they were meant for a funeral. I told him you must have ordered them online from some expensive florist in Paris. He dismissed me as if I were an idiot. These fresh flowers couldn't have come from Beijing.

Twenty-six years into our marriage, Michel is still torn about our anniversary. Let's attend a concert and celebrate, I suggested last week. The doctor will be glad to discharge me for just one night. I read about a sexy Chinese pianist who wears a sequin bikini onstage and plays Bartók with the best orchestra in the world. She graduated from our conservatory. She is coming to town. We can have a nice Italian dinner afterward. Let me take care of our tickets and restaurant reservation. What use is there for such Hollywood romance? he said, and gave me that exhausted look: Haven't I given you enough? Haven't you been telling your darling sister in Beijing how I dote on you?

Yes, indeed. Didn't I say in passing I couldn't live without him?

And you too—that is what sisters are for, or so I thought.

Please write. Yours,

May 16, 2016

Dear Su,

A letter arrived three days ago. It was addressed to Michel. One sentence said it all. The handwriting was tiny and awful: characters diminishing by the line, squeezed together in a downward slant. I don't understand.

No, I can't. How could you possibly have Parkinson's? How long has the condition been diagnosed? The conservatory must have fired you after the spring break. Why didn't you say something? Where is our Motherland when you need her?

Tell me if you are seeking treatment now. I have been vomiting since your news reached me. I don't know how you cope with this hell with no one by your side. I have lost my appetite and drink only water. I eat air, Michel complains. Like an anorexic. We three are in our mid-fifties.

May 26, 2016

Dear Su,

Michel is convinced that you have never forgiven me. Being ill does not exorcise anything. Is that why you never visit or write me even when I am hospitalized? You and I are ill now. What are we still waiting for?

They upped my dose this morning. I haven't lost my mind, I told my doctor. No one believed me, not even Michel. The symptoms of psychosis were related to trauma, one of the nurses said. I was in an altered state yesterday.

After lunch, they transferred me to another ward. Michel wasn't informed about the paperwork. I prefer my new room, smaller but cozier, the window looking out on one of the gardens in the compound. A siren goes off every now and then. It doesn't bother me. I am listening to Shostakovich's Prelude for Two Cellos. The piano is imposing. I prefer the piece unaccompanied. The bed next to mine is empty for now.

Please write.

Yours,

June 6, 2016

Dear Su,

I couldn't protest at the Chinese embassy at avenue George V this year. Suppose I requested one night's leave to celebrate our wedding anniversary, and a day out for the Tiananmen commemoration?

Was I aware that a hospital wasn't a hotel? Michel went on my behalf—he would have gone anyway. He told me afterward that only a handful of people were present outside the entrance. The same few faces, he said. Ying, Tong, and Lou showed up. As usual, they kept to themselves. Three musketeers. Still single. There were few reports in the media. Michel refused to give me the details. Numbers dwindle after twenty-seven years.

You could have left with us after the massacre. Michel would have found you a visa too. What had the country promised you until then? We did not betray you, Su. I am your flesh and blood. I had never thought of stealing Michel from you. He slept with me in the square because you gave him no reason to hope. He loved you—he still does. He has stayed with me out of guilt. He stays with me because I am your twin sister, your substitute.

He never understood why you rejected the movement from the outset. Neither did I. There was no going back for us after the hunger strike. Our friends did not fight for nothing. Believe me, they did not die for nothing.

June 16, 2016

Dear Su,

Michel visited me after lunch and we took a stroll in the garden. This is my third week at Hôpital Sainte-Anne. He told me how you two first met at the Beijing Hotel, a coincidence—that you made conversation in the lounge and wound up spending the night together. Yes, I remember, I said, to his surprise. That was in February, before the student movement picked up steam. How unthinkable it was then that our lives would forever change in a matter of weeks. Until now, he had no idea that you waited for me at the train station after sneaking out of his hotel room at five A.M. I recalled your voice in pieces, how it trembled while I tried to make sense of what you were saying. Why were you terrified? Was it because you did not brace for love? I alighted from a night train with my cello. I had played the worst Bach and Haydn of my life. This was the first time we did not perform a duet together—I was chosen for a concert in Tianjin, without you. On our bus to the train station, I told Teng the local piano accompanist that my career as a cellist was over before it had even begun. Teng did not hide his thoughts from me. He told me that he was asked to submit a report about my conduct. I was coming back to Beijing.

June 26, 2016

Dear Su,

My migraines paralyze me. They haunt me as much as the massacre. I don't understand—someone in the ward told me the lilies were from Michel. They lasted a little over a week. I broke the vase. Who threw the flowers away without telling me?

I have been seeing things and can't sleep. I feel groggy. The corridor in our ward seems to be shrinking by the day. Every night feels like a countdown. I am getting confused. The music has stopped in my head. I can't control my hands. What are they doing to me? I beg you to write. Yours,

July 6, 2016

Dear Su,

I love these pictures of the Lama Temple. Michel showed them to me yesterday. Who took them? How I wish you had jotted down some thoughts behind one of them: a note or poem or something . . . anything to tell me you are fine. Who is the tall and fit mustachioed man behind you in these photos—hair ruffled and in distinctive green military uniform and five-star headgear—holding a cigarette in one hand and a rolled-up newspaper in another? He is frowning, and so are you. He reminds me of the bachelor son of Old Madame Shao from Shanghai, who retired and moved into our building that summer . . . Both mother and son must have been assigned to keep an eye on us.

Are the eighteen luohans, the life-size arhats, still there, in the Hall of Eternal Harmony? I recall them each in a unique sitting position, meditating with various dramatic hand gestures. In their state of nirvana, their faces appeared to me in dreams. The doctor wanted me to put them on paper when I woke up. Keep a diary, Dr. Pascal said. I promised I would try, although I couldn't concentrate. Some arhats looked ferocious, like warriors at the kill. One was bald-headed and had bushy eyebrows. He smiled with his dark brown lips pursed and bent down to talk to me in a thundering voice that echoed: *You're in a wicked world, full of sins and greed. Did you steal your sister's hawthorn berry candy stick when she was taking a nap? Yum yum* . . .

Before each arhat, the locals burned colorful joss sticks in bundles that were thicker than our wrists. They prayed aloud the mantras out of piety and hit their heads against the ground. They prayed for rebirth, a better reincarnation. Plates of cooked vegetables and meat bun offerings rot after days, flies buzzing atop.

Smoke rushed into our faces while incense sticks burned, and we shivered in the cold and fear. We were seven. What did we know of the future? It was late autumn and pouring outside. We ran from the prayer wheels behind the Hall of Eternal Harmony, where we had spun the wheels with all the strength we could muster and however we liked, after sticking empty coiled papers onto them. No words, so no prayers and no message, no reward from Heaven.

Yes, I remember. Floors in the hall were slippery. They were covered by shattered tiles. Their turquoise—was it the imperial blue?—had long since faded. Yet, we ran like beasts up and down the ancient hall, playing "the bandit catches a poor girl." You usually wanted to be the bandit. Back home at night, we begged our mother for horror stories, but covered our faces in tears once long-haired ghosts without eyes appeared in the plot and the scene turned bloody. Never once, when I gave up and stopped running, fell on my butt on the muddy wet tiles, weeping in protest, would you not take me into your arms, caress my hair, and softly sing to console me: *Let me protect you, I won't leave or betray you, O never and never, my dearest Ai, my jiejie . . .*

July 16, 2016

Dear Su,

Have you tried acupuncture?

Please find someone to do some exercise together. Do you practice tai chi in the morning? Michel does. He has joined a group that meets twice a week in Jardin du Luxembourg. I know he prefers not to work out with me. He doesn't want to lose face in public when I can't control my movements or anger. Before he comes by for an afternoon visit, I play Frisbee in the hospital garden with two Arab-speaking patients from my ward. I don't know what their mental disorders are, but they let me win. They seem interested in me. No one practices tai chi or qigong in the hospital. Should I tell Michel that there are rumors that patients sleep with one another when they get out of here?

I miss you, sister. Michel doesn't love me the way he used to. I don't blame him. He says you are fine. God knows what *fine* means. Are you allowed to play cello at home? He has been dodging my question. He doesn't trust my memory.

Has he been hiding your letters from me?

July 26, 2016

Dear Su,

Parkinson's could be hereditary, said a senior nurse. Dementia comes next. Apparently Parkinson's is related to a number of "environmental factors," including frequent "exposure to pesticides." It affects the elderly most.

Why is it happening to you?

Can traditional Chinese medicine help? Let me ask Michel to look up online Chinese physicians in your district.

Write, please. I will wait for your news.

Yours,

P.S. I found an article by an American poet. He wrote: One becomes more vulnerable to Parkinson's when stress and trauma are internalized. *Say nothing. Don't confront problems. No conflicts.* Parkinson's is therefore a loose word for denial.

August 6, 2016

Dear Su,

Michel said he could not bring me pictures anymore. Dr. Pascal didn't think it was a great idea. I can't imagine how Beijing has changed over the years. Have you passed by Xicheng District recently? Is the conservatory located at Baojia Street as before? I think of the tree-lined lanes around hutongs, dead-end alleys parked with bicycles and mobile noodle vendors, and students squatting in twos or threes to wolf down their greasy pork pot stickers with soup and steamed buns. Last month, I heard on the radio about the rampant demolition of hutongs. Several Beijingers were interviewed in the street. One blamed the Dutch and Germans for aggressively investing in a high-rise mall. Come what may, foreigners are outsiders.

Do the minders still follow you wherever you go?

Who is he? The man in those Lama Temple photos?

August 16, 2016

Dear Su,

I know they have never stopped punishing you for what Michel and I did that summer. Michel recalled someone following him at the Beijing Hotel at the time. A pretty Chinese woman in her middle years with hair reaching her waist followed him into an elevator the morning he checked out of his room. Quickly she struck up a conversation with him. Funny, I thought, that the authorities sent a woman instead of a man. What did they have in mind? Michel did not tell me what happened next. It never crossed my mind that you might have something to do with her. I should have asked.

Have you forgotten your secret meetings with Michel at the Beijing Hotel? The more questions I ask, the more I doubt our past. Even yesterday feels so far removed from me. I am in a nowhere land. The medicine has kicked in by now, Michel said. He left for an assignment in London last night.

I am anxious to hear from you. Will I ever see you again?

Affection,

August 16, 2016

Dear Su,

Where is your cello now?

Dear Su,

I didn't sell mine.

August 26, 2016

Dear Su,

Michel brought some books, mostly crime novels. He wonders how I kill time. I told him, I don't. Time passes without making a scandal. Sometimes it just runs out. He photocopied a poem about the Lama Temple. I have copied it out a few times to learn the first verses by heart:

> *in northern winter*
> *on straitened boulevards with leaves in the air*
> *before the Buddha of beauty and wisdom*
> *few times I want to cry*
> *but hold tears back*

Michel pointed out that I translated the poem a few years ago. I can't remember a thing now. Since when did I work as a translator? After I decided to give up cello for good, he replied. He reminded me I was a poet myself. Am I still a poet? I asked. And I denied, No, I've never met this Chinese poet in person . . .

True, we never met, but Michel corrected me, we spoke once on the phone—briefly, because her twin daughters were crying in another room. She is a rising star who married a rock singer and writes about sex. She too is a Beijinger. Su, do you know her? Surely you must have come across her work online . . . I should have introduced you two. Michel said she phoned last week to ask how I was.

a middle-aged woman finishes her mobile call
heaves a soft sigh
holds up three joss sticks
bows her head deep down
a thick gold necklace
rows down her chic leather collar
to her pale fleshy neck

Michel reminded me that the Chinese poet and I got along. We enjoyed reminiscing about old Beijing, he said. She was fluent in French and a fan of Duras. I can't recite the verses anymore now. Words slither away from me after I write them out. They are swimming on the sheet of paper. I cover them with pictures of the Lama Temple—

I feel a sudden chill
cower, bury my face in my hands sob aloud
people come forward to pay respects
in hasty footsteps
striding over my body heavily
surging on, kowtowing like mud

I have never had a "thick gold necklace" or a "chic leather collar." Who is the middle-aged woman in this poem?

Dear Su,

I tore up the paper. The nurse rifled through my belongings. She confiscated the books and magazines. I was writing on the wall when she arrived. I wanted to copy out the poem one last time.

Dear Su,

Michel asked me if the hospital was oppressive. I repeated, *Op-pres-sive*. The word sounded friendly, I had heard it before. I knew what that meant, I replied. I couldn't wrap my mind around it, even though I understood what it meant. More words rushed into my mind. *Mi-chel*, I repeated. But I just couldn't recall my name.

September 6, 2016

Dear Su,

I looked at myself in the mirror after lunch. I was as skinny as a luth. I didn't look myself at all—I wished I had dyed my hair before Michel admitted me. It has been months since I saw my hairdresser. How exhilarating to take a vacation from an old self.

Can you please send a picture of yourself? I can't stop seeing you as a child. My imagination is playing tricks on me. I can't remember how you looked when we left Beijing. Did we even say goodbye? I write everything down now. Dr. Pascal said writing could help.

Dear Su,

Where did I keep the clean copies of Offenbach's duos, opus 52?

September 16, 2016

Dear Su,

Mid-autumn—

Our favorite moon festival!

I told Michel to order five boxes of mooncakes, each with four mooncakes and of a different flavor, from a Chinese Vietnamese bakery in Chinatown. All twenty mooncakes arrived by noon— lotus seed paste with salted egg yolks, red bean paste with sliced melon seeds, and my favorite: five kernels, nuts, sugared winter melon, and dry-cured ham from Jinhua. I hid some under my bed. When we were kids, you had a soft spot for those with golden brown baked crusts and the ones with frozen crystal rice crusts. I am watching the moon tonight.

September 26, 2016

Dear Su,

I am hallucinating conversations. I told the doctor, I was being tuned in to and out of others' lives, as if I were a radio and its voices all at once. Dr. Pascal said nothing. The nurse asked for my permission to switch to another treatment.

    I can't write. Love,

Dear Su,

Please write. Love,

October 6, 2016

Dear Su,

Are you staying at home most of the time?

    I told Dr. Pascal I wanted a new room. A room with more character, I insisted. My words seemed to have taken him by surprise. He said, Let's see how things go this winter. I found out that he had started me on L-dopa since last month. The voices were real after all. The shadows were real. So were you. You told me not to get too close and accused me of being an impostor.

Dear Su,

I told Dr. Pascal I must change my room tonight. Once I lay in bed, it started to shrink and float above my feet. My bed moved twice and I was frozen in it.

Michel phoned the hospital. He said he was coming.

Come please, sister.

Dear Su,

Michel said you take tranquilizers and cannot answer the phone. He brought me butter cookies. I wanted banana ice cream. He told me you were in a nursing home. I pray that you are rid at last of those silent watchdogs.

October 16, 2016

Dear Su,

When did you last dance or sing?

Again, no word from you—

Michel brought me pop music for a change this morning. He seemed relieved. I have been feeling much better. I am excited. The disc contains only happy songs, he reassured me. I haven't heard of this Tibetan pop singer who sings in Chinese, I said. How to pronounce her name? I was thrilled by this discovery and asked Michel to google her on his iPhone. But there was virtually no information about the singer beyond the disc listed. The same few pictures of her in traditional Tibetan clothes circulated on the internet, and that was it.

Here she is, Michel showed me another image. She stood on a

cliff, looking out over the sea, in a black chuba robe with pants under a silk apron and ribbon, and a golden scarf with a dragon motif. Is this Chinese or Tibetan tradition? I asked. Is she an impostor?

I zoomed in the picture. Her gaze turned inward and outward at once. I couldn't help being obsessed by her looks. She seemed quite sophisticated for a Tibetan folk singer. How shallow—you used to scold me for judging people by appearance. Even as a child, I judged the arhats.

Michel claimed that he'd met this singer before. Sure, I muttered under my breath. For sure, he confirmed, grabbed my left arm, and stared at me.

October 26, 2016

Dear Su,

Now I remember. The Tibetan singer was one of your colleagues at the conservatory. Has anyone from work kept in touch with you since you fell ill? What about your students? I hope they haven't forgotten about you. I know how it feels to be forgotten. It's like getting lost in the Hall of Eternal Hell.

Dear Su,

I can't sleep. I haven't slept since the night you came for me in the square. The students were outnumbered, but the crackdown had begun. The stun grenades must have struck me down. I couldn't see. I should have followed you home instead of running away.

Dear Su,

I plan to ask Michel for Adele the next time he comes. Taylor Swift works too. Listening to a voice singing in English is easier than one chanting in Chinese or Tibetan or both. My headaches hinder me from thinking straight. I don't know how to relax. I can't open my eyes.

November 6, 2016

Dear Su,

Our ward stank of cigarettes and garbage last night. I arrived at the square once I left my room. My neighbor Saiko told me she smelled whiskey and marijuana. Later, she told me that I smelled of strawberries. My hands played on cello strings before I slept. I couldn't find a bow. The stage was empty. The background music grew louder, but my cello disappeared into my body before I finished the second movement.

Saiko said she found my tune comforting but melancholic. Then her lips moved, I couldn't hear her anymore. She did not look sad so much as I felt empty. I'm telling you because she wore your pajamas. She also peed in bottles at night. The first stroke paralyzed half of Saiko's body. It affected her speech. Saiko was born in Osaka and came to study in Paris ten years ago. She worked for a German rare book collector at rue Dauphine, in exchange for lodging and meals. But she was found homeless after the German book collector had passed away, and she suffered a series of mental breakdowns. Saiko has been hospitalized since last spring and transferred twice in and out of my ward. I couldn't tell if she was still the same person inside. I didn't know how to ask her. A Vietnamese woman visited often.

Michel joined me for lunch today. He bought noodles and fed me. When he stroked my hair, his hands trembled. Something was wrong with him. I told him about the locust trees in the corridor. He said they were still there—along Baojia Street in Xicheng District.

November 16, 2016

Dear Su,

Saiko invited me to her room. We watched Italian films together. You must watch Antonioni and Pasolini, she told me. I had watched them with my German lover.

I never liked them, I said. Men were cruel and perverse in those films. But that was their real nature, she stammered.

In one scene, a group of Fascist officers arrested several beautiful young women in the middle of the street. They stripped them naked, then forced them to open bottles of whiskey and serve them food. The women stared into the camera. They shivered in the cold and began to weep.

Another silent scene: A lover slapped his mistress, threw her onto the bed, then undressed her—in all tenderness—with his teeth and a turned gaze. The couple groped in the dark, in slow motion; on the bed, the woman curled up into a fetal position, as if grimacing with a smile. A nausea came over me.

I complained about Saiko to Dr. Pascal and the nurses. I told them her mind was sick. I told them not to let her come near me.

November 26, 2016

Dear Su,

I want to reread the letters I wrote you. Can you send some back to me?

I don't mean to ask that you return them. Just send a few photocopies. I won't tear them up, I promise. Please also send a transistor if possible. Michel took away my music.

Dear Su,

Is it too much to ask for some music?

Dear Su,

I left sheets of Handel's Sonata in G minor in my cello case. They were notated. I also scribbled on our music stand: the first two bars of a Ravel piece. I hadn't finished adapting the violin part for a second cello.

Dear Su,

Saiko is bothering me again. She said Mussolini ordered secret government agents to abduct his illegitimate son and intern him in an asylum like ours. The son was murdered at twenty-six. His nurses injected him with an overdose of antidepressants. Did you and Michel lock me up here?

December 6, 2016

Dear Su,

I don't understand. They said my mind has slipped away from me. It's normal—that's Parkinson's, Michel kept assuring me. Did you have a similar experience? Michel said, Michel said . . .

He wept for the first time. He looked wan.

I asked if he had been overworking. He said he had lost me since a while now. I wasn't sure if he apologized. I was certain he talked about you. He kept saying that you never existed. What have you told him of late?

Dear Su,

I see a pagoda of heads. The square tilts into a giant bowl. Lights are blinding me while faces close in. Someone has moved a TV next to my bed.

Dear Su,

A voice tells me you don't exist.

  She is dead, the voice dictates. She's been dead for years. Someone is making my past up along the way. Who decides what is right or wrong? Dr. Pascal tells me I am doing fine on a dose of saline. Yes, his voice . . . I can't see him clearly. The window keeps moving. He asks me, Who is Su?

  Yours,

December 16, 2016

Dear Su,

It is getting cold in Paris. How about Beijing?

  Be gentle with yourself. Wait for me. I am doing my best. Michel says no one cares about the massacre anymore. No one cares about the past. I reply, I do, you do.

December 26, 2016

Dear Su,

There are minders now in my room.

NEWS FROM SAIGON

1995–1996

"That's enough." I pushed away the drunk client with the clammy hands and edged past him through the bathroom door, back into the bistro, deserted on a Monday morning. Marguerite had arrived while I'd been working. We said our bonjours but nothing else. Down the narrow lane, even Les Deux Magots and Café de Flore, the oft-trodden cafés of Saint-Germain-des-Prés, were empty of their privileged patrons from various corners of the world. Unlike the Parisians, these visitors spoke in a medley of languages, as if waiting for the aficionados of Sartre and Beauvoir to surface from nowhere. I never went to Les Deux Magots or Café de Flore. I was not welcome there. They were too highly regarded for the likes of me.

Here at Le Petit Saint-Benoît, Thierry the blond garçon was working the morning shift. In tan jeans and a plain checkered shirt, he whistled and mooned around the tables. Unsurprisingly, he pretended that Marguerite and I weren't there.

She sat on the far end of the bar, against the wall. When she finished her whiskey, she pushed the glass away in one swift motion before moving her scrawny hand up against her face. A Chinese jade bangle hung loose around her wrist. She furrowed her brow and moved her lips as if she were mumbling words to herself. Did she try to act disinterested or was she truly indifferent? Lonely, I thought. In her other hand she grasped a fountain pen with all five fingers. The pen, a vertical body, suspended and alert. She held it like a knife.

She'd been coming to the bistro almost every day for a few weeks now, but I couldn't possibly know who she was. I could neither read nor write and couldn't be happier not to do either. Her eyes hidden behind somewhat largish and thick dark-rimmed eyeglasses, she kept her gaze low. Yet I felt it: it ate at my skin when I stared too long from the side of my eyes. She was a petite and fragile old woman bundled up in an oversize fur coat. Was she even five feet tall? Her legs hung suspended in the air, the wooden barstool high above the maroon-tiled floor. Her feet didn't even reach the bar rail. Her hair was short and close-cropped, with streaks of grays just above the ears, combed backward on both sides, no bangs but a discernibly wrinkled forehead—the neat, masculine profile of a former prima donna. Out of proportion, bigger than usual, the head and its double chin weighed oddly on her body, as if she had no neck. No smile, no squirm. I couldn't help but take her for a bulldog—a fake bulldog on a window display, dressed up and stuffed inside an expensive faux fur pillow.

"*Elle ne veut pas être dérangée,*" Thierry hissed in my ear, pressed up against me from behind. *She doesn't want to be disturbed.*

"Sure," I answered, not meeting his eyes. But I sensed his scorn, so I fired back nonchalantly, "What makes you think I wanted to disturb her?"

I spoke loud enough for her to hear. I was hoping she would turn around. She did not. Two bicycles sprinted down the street outside Le Petit Saint-Benoît after turning right at the street corner from rue Jacob. Thierry scowled. Dismissively he picked up his whistling and made a dart for the door behind the bar, as if I had said nothing and he had not heard a word.

In the old woman I saw myself. Would I end up resembling her? Thinner, no doubt, and younger, but I was, like her, small and uninspiring. Who would lay eyes on me, much less notice my presence from afar? Even in the bistro I felt myself melt into the cacophony, the amber walls, patches of dated paint peeling off around the border of vintage posters and mirrors, plates and salad bowls, those glass mugs that each held a liter, paper mats with alternating crimson and white checks . . . In every mirror, I showed boredom, a blanched face with watery eyes and parched lips. When I was a child back in Saigon, my mother used to complain, *Look at you, an up-and-coming heroin addict*.

I wasn't on a diet—I didn't need one—but only the vodka held me together at this hour in the morning. At last I caught her eye. After all, I was the real exotic one, wearing a dirty pale cream ao dai and fanning away at myself. I sat at the bar on the toilet side, game to disappear behind the door with any man I could get close to. Like her, I knew how to seduce.

"Anything else?" Thierry came back out of the kitchen, this time dressed in his black and white waiter suit, a tray balanced on his left shoulder. He was ready for work.

I shook my head. My stomach twisted and I almost winced. Hunger was the best discipline for women, bragged my friend

Berta, a veteran cancan dancer who hailed from Bonn and used to work at Montmartre. She had a wealthy family and came to Paris to pursue sculpture. Recently, Berta performed at Le Crazy Horse, a cabaret in Champs-Élysées. She danced to rebel against her family, their bourgeois class. Not for me, I contradicted Berta squarely one night. She didn't know hunger, I thought; that was self-deprivation. Hunger ran through my body, more like waves of menstrual pain and worse than tides of insomnia.

The grande dame broke the ice.

"*Donnez-lui ce qu'elle aimerait*," she said. *Give her whatever she likes.* The pen dropped flat on the table. She managed a simper and continued to tinker with the jewelry on her left hand: an ostentatious silver ring with gemstones and an intricate design on each finger except the thumb and index finger.

"Vodka," she chimed in, and her husky voice rose, "or opium. That's what our mademoiselle really wants."

The next morning, Thierry moved us to a table opposite the counter.

"Madame"—he glanced at Marguerite and spoke furtively—"you'll have more privacy there. No one else is in that corner."

We were sitting several stools away from each other, with a large red stain on the floor and scattered pieces of glass under the table. A fight had taken place in the bistro before she came in for breakfast. What exactly happened, I couldn't remember. I had been behind the toilet door, a Monsieur Oster rocking me away above the sink. He stuffed a few hundred francs into my right stocking while I kept stroking him with two of my fingers until his upturned face froze and he moaned. At the end I didn't even realize about my torn stockings and fatigue. It was Thierry who woke me up.

I asked for a heavy breakfast—whatever that was left over from the night before, I grunted. Thierry gave me a look: I know why you're starving. I poured the mug of beer down my throat, then gulped down the mixed lentil salad he shoved in my face. Delicious. The tomatoes were firm, the potatoes tender and buttery. Impulsively, I soaked the last piece of bread in the beer and put it into my mouth. Like an acidic sauce, it tasted so bitter and sour at once that it numbed me right off. I forced myself to eat slowly. In the background, the radio was playing Archie Shepp.

She ordered *un demi*. "Thuy," she said as she drummed her fingers on the table and waited for her drink, "is a very Vietnamese name."

"And Marguerite," I quipped, "is very French, *n'est-ce pas?*"

Spontaneity and cheekiness were qualities I took pride in—distance as well. I spread the vinegar thin on my plate with the back of a dessert spoon.

She flashed me a crotchety smile. "Well, you must have done a great job last night. You don't seem that unhappy after all."

Silence. I cringed a little. What did this woman want?

"Moreover," she said, as if determined for some reaction, "you seem to have someone who helps you screen clients."

Thierry stole a glance at me. I stared blankly at my food.

"*Alors*, do you enjoy what you do?" She casually drew out a cigarette. Her voice was low and grainy, as if cracking into fragments or bleeding to its end.

"It depends," I said. "Not all men are mean. Some are kind to me."

My own candidness surprised and disconcerted me. I blushed. As a rule, women never spoke to me—they shunned me from afar—especially older women. I had gotten used to it.

"Kind?" She tilted forward to probe again.

I nodded, ignoring Thierry's suspicion. "By the way, *that* is not something I *do*, it is *work*. Money, you get it?" I snapped at her. "And you?"

"I drink," she replied, unabashed. "*That* is what I *do*."

I looked up to search out Thierry, expecting his disapproving glare, but he had sneaked into the kitchen behind the counter. I was on my own. She caught my agitation and turned around to confirm Thierry's absence.

"And I write," she proceeded with an air of composure. "That is my work, mademoiselle. *Alcohol is a substitute for pleasure though it doesn't replace it.* I dictated this sentence to a tape recorder, and wrote and rewrote it. And more—"

"Write as in inventing stories?"

"*Parfois*," she responded curtly—sometimes—and went back to reciting her lines: "*When you've had too much to drink you're back at the start of the infernal cycle of life. People talk about happiness and say it's impossible. But they know what the word means.*"

"What kind of stories?" I was curious, even though I had no idea what she was reciting. My mother's face drifted into my foggy mind, along with her turquoise silk dress, our rice fields, the oxcarts, the sun and monsoon rain, the smell of home-cooked food—steaming pork bones and fish balls in spicy vermicelli soup, the tofu taste of congealed duck and pig's blood in cubes—those bright flame trees, the folktales she told me to lull us both to sleep . . . She a young mother, in happy spirits and health . . . before we took to the road for a safe house in Da Nang, followed by a trawler for a new life in France. We slept in the steerage. On the journey, my mother began to take on work in an upper deck. Men came in and out of a smoggy four-berth stateroom, where she earned her living. As of then, my mother avoided eye contact with me. I did the same to her.

Indochina and the sea seemed light-years away now. It was in Saigon where I first smelled coffee, but in Paris where I first tasted it.

"Any kind," Marguerite replied in a dry tone. "Take yours, for instance. Where do you come from? Who are you? What do you do in life? Why this work? Each question paves the way for a story . . . How I write, how a story is framed isn't the interesting bit; the story juices itself up when I start drinking. That's the tipping point, the moment when I pin down the voice of a story."

She changed the subject and continued, "*Vous parlez bien français*, you speak good French. Why don't you find something decent to do?"

"Decent?" I choked. "For instance?" Both of us might have intuited where this conversation would lead.

"A maid, a student, a bar girl, a receptionist, a mistress . . ." She rattled off a mental list before looking straight into my eyes. I did not flinch.

Suddenly she chortled in a strange laugh that was short and throaty. "*Ma chère*," she said, "you and I are so alike."

*

In the sepia photo, Marguerite was smirking at the camera.

Her lips were luscious and painted. They stayed closed, though neither tight nor tense. Like pencil sketches, her facial features were airy and thinly drawn. The gaze was firm yet vulnerable. The longer I stayed with her glare, the more she looked *through* me, holding my gaze and absorbing it over and over again. It seemed the start of an erotic transaction, an aloof exchange of intimacy that needed no words. She possessed an otherworldliness, an intactness, a visual composition of confidence that hinged on emotional removal.

This was the face and image Marguerite wanted the world to see as her. *After a hundred years they're as brittle as glass,* she remarked about photos. Like this picture, her grace was stopped in time and walled off from age. The smile especially—its uncharacteristic allure, the sort that could draw one in, steadily yet totally. It hid itself, discreet and coy, while craving to be seen.

"Madame, you're beautiful," I whispered, gawking at the portrait.

Was it by a slip of the tongue that I called her Madame instead of Marguerite? Why did she decide to show me the photo? My voice quivered, but I spoke the truth: She was exquisite—youthful and shall I say, innocent?—and to my astonishment, more Asian-looking than I had in mind.

"Was this taken in Saigon?" I asked, and thought of how white men eyed her with desire, how the local Vietnamese and Laotian men lusted after her in a mix of fear, arousal, jealousy, and shame while she, despised by wives and other young women, lured them only as far as arm's length. That was how her seduction and fiction played out. I could picture her mastering the art and manipulation.

Writers, Marguerite spilled a few days ago—unannounced and with some self-disdain—weren't much different from whores: they sold stories like their bodies, all the more when the stories were not theirs to claim.

"I was sixteen in this photo," she muttered, shifting her gaze in another direction. Thierry arrived with a timely glass of cognac. She reached for it. With a smug blink, she declared in a slow drawl, "But I had lovers . . . I was already along in years."

It comforted me to see Marguerite each morning, especially after a difficult night. I had gotten used to her. She was far from maternal—in fact, the way she talked, detached yet certain of herself, came across as condescending and morose—but I enjoyed our complicity. She knew who or what I was and didn't care to judge. I wasn't intimidated by her frostiness. We must have allowed each other to feel forgiven in the wreckage and solitude of our own making. It had been some months since we first spoke to each other. Although she spoke as precisely and as little as before, she smoked and drank more. She had been coughing too. Thierry, on the other hand, had been staring at me more and serving me larger portions of my breakfast order. At some point, I caught Marguerite swallowing pills with her martini.

"What are those?" I said, breaking our rule of silence.

We never spoke about her life or fame—her books, men, admirers, films, rehearsals, insomnia, or alcoholism. Scenes came up fleetingly when she grouched against so-and-so from the press who insinuated that she was *difficile* or *sénile*. What we mostly spoke about were the trivialities, stereotypical anecdotes of women's and men's obsession with one another and, occasionally, my childhood in Vietnam, by now nebulous even to me. "Any news from Saigon?" was what she said when she decided to talk. On her more enthusiastic days, she conversed with me in Vietnamese. Saigon emerged as more her birthplace than mine. I no longer recalled the river. What recollections could I afford from the displaced past of a girl who learned firsthand about sex through her own mother? I offered. And Marguerite would rebuke me: *That*, lies and hallucinations included, was what writing was about. The shaping of a train ride from Hanoi—was it bleak? Yes, it had to be. The recasting of roles in a pimp and a newly arrived civil servant—how did they cross paths? Did they play together when they were children? The girl in the story—the protagonist—could choose to do more and not say much.

"My pills," Marguerite growled. "Meant to cure some disease. I don't have a name for it. Twelve or fifteen years ago, I can't quite remember, I called it *La Maladie de la mort*, The Malady of Death. I was so proud of this byname that I used it later as the title for one of my novellas."

I didn't understand, I said. She shouldn't drain a bottle of pills down her throat with liquor, I insisted.

Marguerite passed over my flummoxed state and continued, "Speaking of books . . ." She slid across the table a small pile of them, wrapped in brown kraft paper. A sly twitch appeared at the corner of her lips.

"What should I do with your books?" I asked up front. I didn't care much for *la culture*—that much, she knew.

"Sell them," she answered with an impassive wave of her hand. "Make some money out of these tattered copies."

She exhaled from her cigarette and waited for my reaction. I was unsure if I should ask more questions or thank her. Still on my feet, I flipped through the books by their covers. Each came with a sparse white design, her name and title printed in blue—she pointed out to me, like a schoolmistress to her student—bordered by a blue rectangle from four sides. I opened one of them: on every page, there were pencil marks in the margins. There were scrawlings within and across the texts too.

The books were signed and dated, their pages read and laboriously underlined. They were her working copies, she said in all seriousness. They smelled of cigarettes. One of them contained an edge indented and smeared by a red blotch. Alcohol.

"Who knows," I spouted. "Ten years down the road, those American tourists from Les Deux Magots or Café de Flore will also swarm here to take pictures, pretending that you are here." Clumsily I tried to trump up a joke to substitute for some measure of gratitude. I almost mentioned Sartre and Beauvoir—not that I knew who they really were—but I stopped my tongue.

"Here? At this bistro where we *work*?" She chuckled. "They don't need to pretend. I'll be here. And you too, I hope."

Autumn had drifted into winter before I dropped by Le Petit Saint-Benoît again. I'd had an abortion—my second—and had sold the books away to a German bibliophile whom Marguerite recommended. There wasn't much of a choice—perhaps Marguerite had foreseen it—I was a few months behind my rent and for weeks couldn't even rouse myself from the bed, let alone work. Berta paid a Filipina living nearby to take care of me. The Filipina maid visited me several times a week. She wasn't keen to make conversation but told me she worked for a Monsieur Fournier at rue Séguier. I did not even know her name. The German bibliophile also lived in the same quartier, but he did not want to meet in person. He sent a courier—a young Japanese student—to retrieve the books before my abortion. The Japanese student—a teenage girl who spoke little French—paid me cash on the German collector's behalf.

"Good grief, I thought I saw a phantom. Where have you been? Où?" Thierry demanded as he glanced up from behind the bar.

His concern took me by surprise. Who could be expecting me? Had there been complaints during my absence? A police investigation?

"I hadn't . . . hadn't gone back to . . . Saigon for vacation, if that was what you imagined." I leaned against the bar counter. I was beginning to feel giddy and out of breath.

Thierry grinned and with his soggy eyes silently ushered me to my usual stool. Boy, he looked different—unshaved, messier hair, swaying and belching at the same time—and as likely as not, so was I, too listless to change out of the clothes I had slept in for a week. It wasn't yet eight in the morning, the city just waking up. The abortion had taken a toll on me. On an empty stomach, I could feel blood draining from my face as I staggered down from my cramped *chambre de bonne* at rue Bonaparte, a street adjacent to the bistro's. What was once a five-minute walk had become a strenuous route uphill. My hands held on any railing and wall along the way before I could sit down at last.

Thierry and me—that was it. A weight sank in my chest.

Gritting a cigarette between his teeth, he switched on the radio and walked over from the sink. I ordered a double espresso and an egg.

"*C'est tout?*" That was all? Loudly he removed saucers from tables, poured leftover coffee from one cup to another, and shuffled teaspoons and forks away onto a tray.

"Two priests walk into a *cinéma* . . ." I purred, trying to cook up a tale. And I was about to drift off on a tangent when without any signal, Thierry thrust me into his arms, stuck his hand up into my bra, and brushed his mouth against mine.

"You think you can come and go as you wish, huh?" He pulled my hair. "How many waiters in this neighborhood allow women like you to lounge around in their cafés? How much longer do you think you won't be caught? Now that your powerful guardian is gone, don't you dare to dream of free food and company without me getting a go at you."

My mind in a blank, I caught his nicotine breath. His beard scratched my face hard and his sweat smeared my neck. Bastard. In a whimper, I bit his tongue before pushing him away and vomiting out the egg.

I had known Thierry would unleash himself on me once we were alone. Why today? No logic, no explanation. I took a good look at him: his back facing me, he was helping an elderly gentleman place his walking cane on a chair, before choosing for him a table near the entrance door. Thierry the garçon, polite as ever. So much for appearance and restraint, they fed violence and made it real. He must have waited long enough to punish me for denying him the chance to *passer à l'acte*, act out his drive and pleasure. How insulting, how nauseating it must have been for a Frenchman, prim and proper, to feed a bony Asian cocotte who made a move on anyone but himself. In a story that Marguerite might have written, her heroine would resist someone like Thierry not out of dignity or in self-defense, but in order for the conflict to succumb to a secret between them. This made sense in books and films in which both parties needed each other to conspire, to fuel the plot, or to lose themselves in their secret. But in the real world, people lost themselves because they believed the secret was always safe with them, duped into thinking the feeling of being lost would be brief and they could come to their senses whenever or wherever they wanted. As I thought of Marguerite, the lines she worked so hard to make real people fictional, I let out a nimble laugh and slipped onto a stool at the other corner of the bar. I took her spot.

Someone walked in. Voices. And more. In my face, Thierry slammed down a copy of the daily *Libération*. A few cups clattered and a plate jumped. I picked up his fury as it zeroed in on my breasts, but I was too weak to be angry at him. *Imbécile*, I said under my breath, yet couldn't be sure if I was blaming him or myself. I took a deep breath and sat on my hands, palms down. Pain seeped from my lower belly to my legs. I shivered. The heater was not working in the bistro. On the front page, the *Libération* featured a portrait photo in colors. My eyes caught the first line of the caption.

I couldn't read the words but recognized Marguerite's name. Then the numbers: her year of birth, hyphen, and the current year, 1996.

A wave of dizziness clawed over my head before I blacked out. Thierry's voice trailed off with the clamor from behind: "*Rien, rien, tout va bien*. Nothing, nothing, all's fine. She isn't ill. Don't crowd in on her . . . I don't want trouble, or the police to come here . . . Please let her get over the shock. It's nothing, really. Her fairy godmother died yesterday."

V

When you grow chrysanthemums
you become a servant
of chrysanthemums

BUSON

DEAR CHRYSANTHEMUMS

1946/1966–1976/1996–2006

I t was the late spring of 1942. Chairman Mao had made his home in the depths of valleys and mountains of Yan'an, in the impoverished province of Shaanxi. There, in a secret lair, camouflaged by birch-leaf pears, wild chrysanthemums, poplars, and willows, he ate peanuts with Huangshan tea, read erotic Ming poetry, and convened a series of Politburo meetings. Behind closed doors, he was launching a human engineering project: *zhengfeng*, Rectify the Wind. Otherwise known as the Rectification Campaign.

"Art for art's sake does not exist in reality," Mao announced from the outset of this campaign, and the same goes for "art that stands above class and party, and fellow-traveling or political independent art." Thus was born a proletarian art, a tool to advocate a "proletariat revolutionary cause." It would take Mao three years to rectify this wind. By the time the wind had subsided in 1945, aesthetics were purged. Mao's writings, their proletarian cause, formed the bedrock of all artistic expressions in the free zones.

Mei was born in the spring after the wind, to a musician and a calligrapher in Shanghai. Like her parents Master and Madame

Zhen, Mei grew up to be an artist to serve the people of Mao's China. She would go where the wind blew her.

Until the Communist liberation, Mei's father worked as a middle-rank Nationalist clerk. He sold stamps, took messages, handled phone calls and paperwork at a local post office. This "problematic background" brought Mei trouble in the heat of the Cultural Revolution: who could know for sure her father wasn't a rightist, a double agent? But Master Zhen's persecution had less to do with his Nationalist background than with the folk musical instrument he'd invented. For fifteen years, he alone had modernized a traditional fifteen-string zither—the guzheng—to a contemporary twenty-one-string instrument twice its original size. Since then, he had been assigned by the city council to found the quasi-nonexistent folk music department at what is now known as the prestigious Shanghai Conservatory of Music. Students traveled miles to take lessons from Mei's father. They came on overnight trains and packed buses, carrying with them planks of wood that passed for handmade duplicates of the plucked string instrument. Most, selected by their municipal schools, came from poor families. They had little to offer but their pure hearts, simple minds, and hard work. Master Zhen always shared his lunch with the students in their canteen and brought them grapes from his garden.

Too young for a proper conservatory, Mei joined the earnest youths nonetheless, and began to learn the instrument under her father's tutelage. She flew a goldfish kite before the conservatory's main gate at recess and gave her first performance at age six in a city hall during the local mid-autumn moon festival celebrations. She played the zither standing. "Harp strings are to me what sushi is to the Japanese," she later boasted to her own students.

Pure hearts, simple minds became the slogan on the streets. Most classmates and musicians turned their backs on Mei after her parents were officially labeled. Rumors spread, gossip bred like weeds and worms. Weeks into the Revolution, no one dared to approach the Zhen family. Classes were suspended across the country. Mei applied to work as a propaganda worker in Beijing. Misfortune followed her north. Passersby spat on her in the streets; even children took to doing so. People grew so used to the pleasure of spitting on her that they continued, even though they had forgotten why.

News reached Mei: two of her father's former students had been promoted to the elite rank of Commandant Red Guards and were now in charge of "working on Master Zhen." When they charged to the Zhen house at Huaihai Middle Road with a horde of thirteen-year-olds brandishing red flags and sickles, even Mei's mother naively thought that her husband's favorite students had come to shield him from harm, the ill winds of the old bourgeois, to rehabilitate a Nationalist clerk.

Mei wanted to return to Shanghai. But the authorities refused to grant her permission. Instead, she was sent down to the remote country in Anhui province for thought reform labor. She was assigned to a camp in the Huangshan area. The work was alien to

Mei: plucking chrysanthemums in the far-flung mountains and drying them in time for peasants from nearby villages, who collected dried flower heads the next day to process them into "top-grade" herbal chrysanthemum tea packs. Mei's assigned quota was five baskets per week.

Life did not exist in these punishing rural cadre schools. Like her other banished comrades who now spent their days plucking chrysanthemums, Mei woke up at four and slept by nine in a pig shack. They ate from baskets of stale dumplings with scant meat fillings, showered twice a week in a nearby stream. They goose-stepped between grueling work shifts and interminable thought reform sessions. They sang patriotic songs, read nothing but soiled copies of the Little Red Book. The women spoke little and mistrusted one another. Every other week they were inspected by anonymous *lingdao*, leaders who came from the prefecture. Whenever Mei failed her quota, she would be detained in the dingy canteen, ordered to write an afternoon of self-examination reports, repeating lines such as "Long Live Chairman Mao" and "Let's pluck chrysanthemums that bloom for our red future."

To stave off boredom, she altered their punctuation—one sentence ended with two exclamation marks, another six—or experimented with varied calligraphic fonts she learned from her calligrapher mother: seal script, clerical script, regular script, semi-cursive, and wild cursive.

But Mei escaped the worst, all because of a piece of music she had composed before the sweeping witch hunt.

*

Mei was sixteen when she wrote *Combat the Typhoon*. It was a composition exercise assigned by her father for his graduating class. At that time, she had been living for some months in the dormitories by the Port of Shanghai, sharing her quarters with the workers. She drew inspiration from the harbor scenes and the emotional weather of the working-class comrades, who had come from villages in outlying counties to work in the city. Mei also invented new guzheng techniques in her debut piece. Instead of plucking the strings with just the right hand, she crossed the left hand over the bridges to produce chords and arpeggios on top of vibratos or dampening effects on the strings from the left. Mei introduced glissandos and tremolos in the music to dramatize in tone-painting the Shanghai quay laborers' combat against forces of nature while protecting the commoners' possessions. The piece was ideologically correct: it celebrated the Chinese working class as prescribed by Mao. It was a fresh take on proletarian art for an ancient instrument, ahead of its time.

Combat the Typhoon became famous overnight in 1962, and so did Mei. She won national prizes and accolades. Her composition explored the virtuosity of both hands and was recognized for its experimental playing techniques. No previous work in Chinese folk music had sought to expand the harmonic range of the guzheng strings beyond two octaves. More crucially, Mei's ode had captured, as described in a Chinese elementary school textbook, the "fearless fighting spirits of dockworkers who overcame catastrophic natural forces with perseverance and inner strength."

*

Chrysanthemums bloom early in the autumn. Noble flowers in Japan, they flourish under short days and long nights. Their petals bear a resemblance to the sun's rays.

In Mei's labor camp, they bloomed because "Chairman Mao drank chrysanthemum" since his *zhengfeng* campaign during the forties and had never ceased to marvel at its healing properties. Winds helped Mao stake an iron-fist claim on the party leadership. He did not care for the flowers' melancholia or their traditional placement at funerals.

For six years, Mei cultivated them and plucked their flowers, but she never believed in their magic.

The women in the camps were ordered to use chemicals when the flowers decomposed upon exposure to heat and light.

The sun massacred their peach chrysanthemums, not the tenderest but the most feminine looking of all.

In 1972, six years into Mei's political reeducation in the mountains, news of Nixon's state visit spread from one labor camp to another. Mei's mission was for her people, in the name of the people: perform *Combat the Typhoon* for Nixon and Mao.

By the time the Politburo and the Central Committee issued orders to liberate Mei, she could no longer rid her capitalist hands of their stench. Over the years, her fingers had hardened with calluses and scars. Her back ached with rheumatism.

Mei was separated from the cohort and given a cadre's room all to herself. A former army cook arrived from the outskirts of Hefei. He began to nourish Mei with duck meat, crab dumplings, ginseng, and longan. Two weeks later, on the instructions of Premier Zhou Enlai, an express night train fetched Mei to Beijing, where she was pampered with balanced nutrition and a heated hotel room "until further notice."

January was the harshest month in Beijing. Plainclothes government agents monitored Mei at a distance. She nursed herself back to health, first by being gentle with her own thoughts. Quietly she waited for music and freedom.

The guzheng arrived from Shanghai. It was Mei's favorite, the one her father made, and the one she had been practicing on since she was eight. She'd helped her father replace plywood with paulownia for its soundboard, rosewood for its frame. Instead of silk, crane bone marrows, deer sinew, or horse mane, the strings were in nylon and steel. Since the persecutions, Mei's parents had hidden her harp in an underground cache behind their compound, by then raided and occupied by unknown migrant tenants. The instrument, unlike a great many looted national treasures, survived the unhinged revolution, and officials were adamant about retrieving it for Mei's performance.

No longer an object of feudalism, the guzheng had found its own freedom. It was rehabilitated by special consent from Madame Mao, now the de facto chief of the Gang of Four, who signed the attestation: "a harmless artistic object, unmarred by Confucian ethics, nonthreatening to our spiritual health."

*

Mei ate, spoke, and slept with the zither while confined secretly in the capital. The room was bare and white and hostile, like the operation theater of a hospital. It was a room from nowhere for people to go nowhere. Room 6, the divine number. The room for someone to disappear. A room to disappear politically sensitive people.

A skeletal silhouette stirred against the wall. Whose ghost? The music she composed couldn't stop in her head.

There was no window.

No mirror.

Newspapers, radio stations, and TV networks reported about Mei's phenomenal typhoon. Her performance was the highlight of the night—the clip that featured Chinese performing artists at their best, undeterred by sufferings from these wanton years. Mei's typhoon music was a metaphor for the ongoing political whirlwind. Nixon was impressed. In a steel posture, the young woman plucked the strings. Notes took flight. Her lips were parched. The strings stayed taut. None broke, but her fingernails did. She had not lost the touch after all. She could still command the soul of a zither.

At a banquet after the performance, Chairman Mao congratulated Mei. He shook her calloused hands—a gesture of heartfelt gratitude from the people, he said—and made her promise to compose a new guzheng concerto. She would base its music on one of his favorite poems, "The Ballad of a Luth" by Tang poet Po Chü-i.

Mei ate shiitake mushrooms and century eggs at the banquet. Guests were served the finest wine in the country, the best tea in Asia. Even Nixon and Kissinger ate with chopsticks and drank chrysanthemum. No one offered Mei the first-rate chrysanthemum. She wasn't allowed to pee when she worked—chrysanthemum was a natural diuretic—so she did not ask for it, either.

Of course Mei knew "The Ballad of a Luth."

She remembered it from an unmounted scroll of calligraphy in her mother's cursive script. It stands to reason that while the Cultural Revolution fanatically strove to "Destroy the Old World, Build a New World," a classical poem by Mao's favorite Tang poet was remarkably exempted from an old world that must be torn down at all costs. "The Ballad of a Luth" was a grand poem about an exiled luth player, the music he played when he first met Po, the poet. As a child, Mei saw her mother struggle with the last quatrain. Not enough *qi*, her mother said, not enough anger.

The girl did not understand her mother, but she watched her finish inscribing the long lyric by heart, in one breath. The ink smudged whenever her mother began a character with a dot or horizontal stroke. Instead of lifting her brush or running it across the mulberry paper, Mei's mother let her ink swell until it became an eyeball on a pale paper. She wrote the text in a running script. Her brushstrokes weren't exactly fast, but they were sharp and juddering. Mei shouted, "Mama, you've dug a grave for every word on your paper!"

The mother ignored her daughter. Instead, she recited the last quatrain: "Then the ice springs congealed with cold, the strings seemed to freeze, / freeze till the notes no longer could pass, the sound for a while cut off; / now something different, hidden anguish, dark reproaches taking form— / at such times the silence was finer than any sound."

Back in Mei's hotel room, the silhouette had vanished, the stillness more woeful. It dawned on her that the silhouette wasn't malicious. Nor was it a figment of her imagination. The spirit was there to see her through the performance. The show was over, so the spirit returned to where it came from. Which in Chinese meant, gone for good but not yet reincarnated.

The Nixon performance did not save her father.

Master Zhen took his life in November, after rounds of humiliation and torture by his former students. Disguised as junior militia officials to denounce their teacher in the streets, they beat and dressed him up as a puppet with a dunce cap. Megaphones chimed the household anthem "The East Is Red," a far cry from the folk music these aspiring artists once elevated. The students printed portraits of Mao en masse and demolished Confucian statues. Children smashed violins, workers burned pianos in the open. The final blow came when the Red Guards took Master Zhen to his hometown in the suburbs of Shanghai and paraded him around. They banged on metal pans, gongs, and drums. A Red Guard, an elite "iron girl" the same age as Mei, shaved half of Master Zhen's head and exposed him naked before the villagers. Some of the locals had lived long enough to know Mei's grandparents and great-grandparents. They had known her father since he was born.

The express night train that fetched Mei to Beijing came for her again in November, this time to Shanghai. She had to collect her father's body, still hanging from an oak tree in Fuxing Park.

Mei moved to New York after the Revolution and disappeared from the public eye. She was never rehabilitated. "I had to petition the authorities for my rehabilitation," she told me at our first meeting in 1996. "And I never did." In her absence, Mei's historic rendition of *Combat the Typhoon* has influenced generations of guzheng players: an inspiration to every boy and girl who dreams of becoming a guzheng star and a young pioneer of the Communist Youth League.

I was one of the young pioneers from the Shanghai Communist Youth League who wore a red neckerchief during the eighties. Tapped to be a top performer, I had spent months rehearsing glissandos and tremolos from Mei's epic piece—a technical requirement for the national Grade Nine diploma in guzheng performance. I couldn't care less for its proletarian spirit, but *Combat the Typhoon* was my weapon. It was a piece I could easily show off whenever I was assigned to give a concert. People were captivated by a seven-year-old girl sitting on phone books on a high chair to reach the height of the zither, its strings sprawling across octaves while her ponytail swayed from left to right. The faster I played, the smarter I thought I had become. At nine, I submitted a term essay on my aspiration. "Well, well," my grandpa said, "go look for Maestro Mei when you grow up." Something in his voice suggested they knew each other. I pressed my mother to find out if they were friends. She brushed my question off and snapped, "Everyone in Shanghai then knew Mei Zhen and her father. They were onetime celebrities."

As it turned out, fate had other plans in store for my career. After my junior high studies in Shanghai, I was spotted at a concert by a talent agent, who signed me on for modeling work in Singapore. I modeled for Gap and Vera Wang. I wore bridal gowns at seventeen, no longer bound by the single-minded pursuit of music. Money lured me to Manhattan: I lived on the Upper West Side and worked long nights in Chelsea from Thursdays to Mondays. A Juilliard-trained pianist rented me her studio before leaving for Paris; she even sent me postcards of Notre-Dame. I met celebrities almost every week. I gave money to an erhu musician in the Times Square subway station. His daughter became my roommate. She urged me to attend church and do aerobics. On Tuesdays and Wednesdays, I dreamed of exotic places such as Angkor Wat while waiting for my paycheck to return to Shanghai. The Russian models kept to themselves, the French and Germans flew home every other week. I was the only Asian girl that season.

I worked in fashion and lived in my own bubble: my heart was pure, the mind simple. I was independent, not yet interested in men or women, but I did not take drugs or smoke, I didn't suffer. I took English classes from Ms. Cloud, a young graduate instructor at Columbia. She came from Singapore and was Shanghainese too. I even had time for French and literature. Cloud's fiancé, Yves, was my French tutor. Life wasn't a bitch, I wasn't unhappy. Yet a sense of loss and incompletion drained me: I no longer belonged to a system, no longer knew what to do with my life. Had I not bumped into a medium in Harlem after a photo shoot one afternoon, I would not have thought of looking up my past. I looked up Madame Mei in the phone directory the next day.

Hello? Yes, speaking . . .

Are you a reporter?

What? Why?

You want harp lessons. Who are you?

Oh. Do you speak Chinese? Come on Wednesday. Ten o'clock. Fifty-eight D Mott Street. D for dog. You don't know Mott Street? Opposite Old Sea, the famous tofu vendor. Chinatown . . . You're Chinese, but you never come to Chinatown?

Don't be late! One hour each lesson. Long-term commitment, do you understand? You must have heart. I mean, set your heart on it. No heart, no song. You can't miss lessons no matter what.

One more thing: do not eat before you come.

Before our first lesson, I went online to do research on *Combat the Typhoon*. I came across a YouTube video of Mei in her twenties, playing her signature piece for Nixon and Mao.

In the video, Mei wears a coral-pink dress with long sleeves, her short hair ending around the chin and in bangs. The dress has a round collar embroidered with a floral strip, buttoned up to her neck. Throughout the recording—six minutes and twenty-five seconds—Mei never looks up from the instrument. Her bearing is dignified while she plays the typhoon with aplomb. Comment boxes under the YouTube video were flooded with emojis and exclamation marks. One viewer identified himself as Donald Duck and posted his comments in broken English: "I would think the composer could jolly well play her piece any which way she so pleased."

Save for recurring headlines in the cultural section of major newspapers from Hong Kong, Singapore, and Taiwan, I found nothing else on Madame Mei and her masterpiece.

Madame Mei kept a large turquoise album filled with newspaper clips in multiple languages. Before a new student or foreign guest, she exuded a wacky mix of warmth and theatricality, exhibiting the album atop her zither, fawning over it in verbal flamboyance as if it were her only child.

"Look at my amazing *Book of Eternal Glories*," she enthused with a wink before passing comments that either shocked or amused the others: "So-and-So is a little vixen! I should have known from her smug look. She put on eBay photocopies of my music scores and sold them to students in the mainland. Without copyrights or my permission, of course!" Or, "See, this is XYZ. Doesn't he look like Robert Redford? Now forty and married with two children. A geologist at Harvard. He kept digging his nose with his left index finger, like an ape, when I was teaching him 'Autumn Moon over the Han Palace.'"

Madame Mei beamed as she pointed at photos on each page of her treasure album. Most of them were passport photos, black and white, and bordered on pride and perfectionism. They represented her protégés—past and present—and the potentials, all to be collected, as if they were mementos of her glories. They made up her empire. Under every photo, a name, year, and geographic region were neatly scribbled in pencil. I figured them as none other than the vital statistics: name, year, and place of birth. After a while, I couldn't but feel a cold shudder. The lines of pictures reminded me of a history lesson when we were taught totalitarianism in Europe: we were shown a documentary that featured photo galleries at the Shoah Memorial of Jewish children exterminated by the Nazis. I swallowed this thought as it sprang to mind.

"There you are, Sky!" Madame Mei cried out. She stopped her finger on a square newspaper clip and lit up, like a child who won a lollipop. My jaw dropped. There was a photo of me at seven years old. It was one of the album's rare color photos. In it, I wore pigtails and polka dots, my eyes red and puffy from my mother's scolding backstage. An ugly brown blotch was smeared across the front of my white dress. The caption was cut off, by accident I assumed, but there I was, unmistakably: my debut solo performance of *Combat the Typhoon*. I was playing at a private garden reception for a tycoon from Hong Kong, who was on a family visit in Shanghai. I had greedily wolfed a third chocolate ice cream before the concert.

I stared at Madame Mei, dumbfounded. The question thundered in my mind, but did not come out of my mouth: how and where the hell did she get my picture? Mei must have read my mind. "No questions now," she said. "Let's start work."

Under Madame Mei's guidance, I learned not to improvise or make up for lost time. I followed rules and stopped flying blind. Note by note, song after song.

"Play Debussy on your Chinese harp," she hammered home, then slapped my shoulders at each beat. "Each note must breathe like summer rain. Haven't you read Tang poets Tu Fu and Li Shangyin?"

"Play cleanly but honor the struggle."

"Make the typhoon last at least five minutes!"

"Put your feet flat on the floor," Mei noted with eyes shut. "The sound floated nowhere. Like a ghost lingering between two worlds."

But, Teacher, I thought, *I created a subtle dampening effect on two lower strings after a sequence of unresolved chords.* Also, how could I tell her why I couldn't put my feet flat on the floor? Rats scurried under the guzheng.

"Too much emotion kills emotion," Madame Mei complained, interrupting my playing. She put down a Styrofoam container of hot wonton soup. "Don't go for the sentimental. State the facts even in music."

Madame Mei was convinced that music must travel. "Your gu-zheng music can't just stay Chinese," she grumbled. "Go global."

Both hands on her hips, the Maestro was proud of her little victory.

"Teacher, let me write about you."

"How—a book? Fiction or nonfiction?"

"I don't know . . . Maybe a play, a film script."

"Who's going to play me? Michelle Yeoh or Meryl Streep?"

After a winter of lessons with Madame Mei, I wrote home to investigate about my picture. How did it show up in Mei's album? I wrote everyone except my mother, but that was not why I paused before picking up the receiver. The phone rang, then stopped. When it resumed, it sounded more prepared for me to answer.

I cut to the chase. "There is nothing for us to say to each other now the truth is out."

"The world is at your feet now. Isn't it, Princess Sky?" my mother hooted. "America must have gotten to your head. Child prodigy, my foot! What mystery did you imagine? I brought you to this world. I gave you music. Were it not for me, how else would you have picked up guzheng when you were little? I was the reason they'd accepted you for Deng Xiaoping's reform talent program at the Children's Palace. You really want to know how many *lingdao* I had bribed? Did you think this obscure instrument fell from the sky and landed in your lap?"

My mother's voice escalated. I bit my lip and refused to retaliate, however tempted I was to ask if she had been in touch with Madame Mei. I felt more repelled by her complicity than my teacher's—both were survivors, their mindsets shaped by their own times; one had a daughter to tidy up her past, the other her student to help reconcile with it. Both women had lived through enough to know better than anyone how to rectify the winds in life, theirs and others'.

"Are you there?" Mother rattled on. "I'm not the one who dug up the past. Now the answers are out in the open, are you satisfied? Do you want more?"

"I've never wanted anyone in our family hurt," I said.

"Hurt? So you've discovered that truth hurt?"

I sighed. "Ma, I just need to know, that's all."

"Says who you *need* to know? The Americans are full of crap, *I know this*, *I know that* . . . all must be said, everything shown. And what do they do with their knowledge after all the curiosity? Nothing! Push a button and the product comes out. *I want, I need* . . . Consumerism, you idiot. It's horseshit! If answers were all that we needed to go somewhere, life would be no more than a vending machine, a convenience store. So tell me, what are you going to do now?"

"I never planned to do anything."

"Liar. You have the answers you wanted, now you think they come free. I'll be the one to pay the price forever—"

"That isn't true, Ma—"

"Why do you keep sighing?" my mother yelled. "Are you ashamed of your mother now that you found out she was a Red Guard?"

I bit my lip harder. Had she been drinking again?

She went on. "Those were crazy times! No one my age lifted a finger to resist. Go against the current? Someone would have turned me in had I disobeyed. We followed Chairman Mao because he told us to. The Chinese rule by the Emperor, you stupid girl. I can't believe how naive you are. We went around helping him light fires. That was what we were taught. Tell the truth, erase the truth, and better yet, spare others the truth—that is how this country works."

"So I'm your weapon and partner in crime?" I muttered between my teeth.

"Shut up. You don't know what you're talking about. What do you know about mass violence? Go ask your grandpa if you don't wish to believe your own mother. Let me say this: You would have done the same. You would have done even worse."

Other than working on Madame Mei's father to his death, what else did you do, Ma? Are you at peace now that Mei has forgiven you and taken in your daughter as her disciple? Atone for our sins if we have a conscience, but do not rake over the past and the errors. I am done with secrets in our family, the past we bury when history isn't credible unless realigned. Go global. Honor the struggle. Move on instead of dwelling on the past. The unresolved chords were quick to slip through my fingers.

We reunited in 2006. When I phoned that summer, I told Madame Mei about my upcoming visit to New York. I too informed her— with some hesitation—of my recent marriage to a Frenchman, our age gap of twenty-six years. Her voice shook with joy and pride. "Marvelous! Fifty-six isn't old . . . who cares even if he were an antique? Isn't our guzheng an antique anyway? We can be sure it's at least several centuries old!"

Madame Mei stayed a spinster all her life. To others, she had spoken of the guzheng as her alter ego, but as a lover or husband, this was the first time I heard. "As long as this man makes you happy, appreciates your talents, and . . ." she continued. The past was not mentioned. We picked up where we left things ten years ago, when I cut ties with her without a word. I had stopped taking lessons after the rift with my mother—how could I bear to face my teacher and guzheng? At first Madame Mei phoned every day, but she stopped trying after a few weeks.

Let bygones be bygones—was that it?

My teacher's enthusiasm made me blush with shame. I couldn't but wonder how she might react upon seeing us in person. A scrawny couple six feet tall with futuristic cat-eye sunglasses. A straw will show which way the wind blows.

On the surface, nothing had changed in Chinatown since September 11—the chaotic jumble, bickering mainland immigrants, gridlocked traffic. Alain and I stood listening to the swish of traffic after an afternoon drizzle, and whiffed the mix of sweat, durians, fish, buses, and trucks. Rows of fruit and vegetable vendors stationed themselves along the main Canal Street, by now part tourist trap, part strip mall, and part demarcation line of downtown New York since the terrorist attack. Some shops had disappeared, but the HSBC bank, jewelry stores, Asian bakeries, and neon shop signs seemed all the same. Even the smells of the neighborhood had stuck around.

We slouched our way through the human traffic and made a turn into Mott Street. Old Mr. Sea the bean curd vendor had retired and moved to Minneapolis. "To enjoy simple joys with his grandchildren," a Chinese granny said to me. She squatted in front of a bakery, gaunt and impatient. No one took an interest in her pirated DVDs. In a twinge of guilt, I bought *The Devil Wears Prada* and *Miami Vice*, two hits that summer. "Gong Li has put on weight in *Miami Vice*," grumbled the granny. She did not bother to thank me or make change. What happened to the fluorescent Taipei teahouse, where I used to buy pork floss and bubble tea? I asked a stranger, who looked up from his cell phone, shook his head, and walked away.

When she first met Alain in early spring in Shanghai, my mother put on her most expensive black velvet cheongsam and smoked a cigar. She nodded but spoke little. I would like to think that language was the barrier. Just as we were prepared to leave her apartment, she stood in the doorway and asked, without looking at either of us, "How much will he receive for his retirement pension?" Alain took a deep breath. "I work as an editor at a small photography magazine," he replied. "We print books, not dollar bills. I might know a thing or two about printing, though."

At the doorway of her studio, Madame Mei overwhelmed us with open arms in her sparkling saffron orange dress and green high heels. Although her hair had grayed, her posture was slightly stooped, she hadn't changed. A brand-new guzheng awaited us as well: it came with a gorgeous bone powder carving of cherry blossoms on well-lustered aged redwood.

"Look!" Madame Mei exclaimed. "The artisan who made it has gone blind. He lives as a recluse near the Lotus Peak in Huangshan. I handpicked the guzheng myself when I was in China last winter. Now destined for you to bring back to Berlin and charm the Germans!" Alain turned to wink at me. Madame Mei had mistaken him for a German, but neither of us corrected her.

We chatted in Madame Mei's rented studio on the second floor of a shophouse at Mott Street. Casually, the Maestro acknowledged having fewer students these days. "My back problem," she said without detour. "The doctor said something about the spinal cord. At least I had made it back in one piece from the labor camp. Sometimes I wake up, asking myself if America was real."

The ceiling, I observed, had begun to leak. A rat scampered across the toilet. We could hear the muffled crowd in the street outside, and from afar, sirens of fire engines and police cars. But Madame Mei's rehearsal space was sparse and tidy and airy. We felt as comfortable here as at an old friend's.

"Have you been to China?" she asked Alain.

He nodded and told Mei about his first visit before the Tiananmen Square massacre. He also mentioned his journalist cousin, Michel, who married a student protester. "He thought she could be happier in Paris," said Alain. "But she's never recovered from the trauma. Her twin sister died looking for her that night . . . near Muxidi, two, three miles west of the square, where the troops had opened fire before midnight."

Mei shook her head. "Nothing's changed in China."

Silence fell on us. The conversation would have turned to the political had it not been our reunion, Mei's first meeting with Alain. She was disappointed also to learn that we did not plan to have children.

"People like me aren't blessed with children," she continued. "I think of Ling and our happy times before the Revolution. Someone found out she was having an affair, but no one knew who her lover was. She never gave me away. We used to travel to isolated villages that had vanished from maps. I was helping my father uncover folk lyrics, record oral histories . . . Even my own parents wouldn't have accepted us if they'd known."

Alain glanced at me. I was at a loss for words. Who was Ling?

"She was probably one of the first of my generation persecuted. She would have become a top ballerina, a superb ballet mistress. No one even knew what happened to her corpse. After my father's death, I tried to find out . . . Someone told me he'd seen her at the Wukang Mansion in Shanghai. But who knows if that was true? If not for music, our guzheng tradition, I too might have taken my own life."

Mei unburdened her secret without a trace of regret. When we set our secrets free, we become orphaned by ourselves and grieve our own death.

She took me into her arms like a long-lost daughter and scrutinized my fingers one by one. Tears glistened in her eyes. I was too embarrassed to put in a word. Truth is naked by nature: when a wind blows at it, it shivers. She must be asking if I had given up music.

"These chrysanthemums are splendid," Alain said, pointing at a pot of flowers on a high pine table. "Where did you find them, Madame Mei?"

My teacher opened her mouth, on the brink of speech, before holding herself back. I reached to touch the golden petals and their fresh lobed leaves. Yes, chrysanthemums, they were still here, poised as a cluster in the same lavender jardiniere from the fifties— not wilted but in full bloom. Why hadn't I noticed them sooner? Madame Mei got up. She plucked the largest chrysanthemum from her bouquet and gave it to us, humming *Combat the Typhoon*.

NOTES

The Chinese figure is from "Asian Figures," translated by W. S. Merwin in *East Window* (Copper Canyon Press, 1998).

The first section's epigraph is after a haiku by Ozaki Hōsai (1885–1926), translated by Makoto Ueda in *Modern Japanese Haiku: An Anthology* (University of Toronto Press, 1976). Katō Shūson (1905–1993) comes from the same source.

Inahata Teiko (1931–2022) is translated by Makoto Ueda in *Far Beyond the Field: Haiku by Japanese Women* (Columbia University Press, 2003).

Natsume Sōseki (1867–1916) is translated by Harold G. Henderson in *Modern Japanese Literature*, edited by Donald Keene (Tuttle/Grove Press, 1957).

Buson (1716–1783) is translated by W. S. Merwin and Takako Lento in *Collected Haiku of Yosa Buson* (Copper Canyon Press, 2013).

The lyrics from "Heirs of the Dragon" by Hou Dejian are from *The Verso Book of Dissent: Revolutionary Words from Three Millennia of Rebellion and Resistance* (Verso Books, 2016).

The verses in "Back to Beijing" are from "In the Lama Temple" by

Yin Lichuan in *Karma* (Tolsun Books, 2020), translated from the Chinese by Fiona Sze-Lorrain.

Alcohol is . . . it, When you've had too much to drink . . . means, and *After a hundred years . . .* are from Marguerite Duras's "Alcohol" and "Photographs" in *Practicalities*, translated from the French by Barbara Bray (Grove Press, 1993).

The verses by Po Chü-i are translated from the Chinese by Burton Watson in "Song of the Lute" from *Po Chü-i: Selected Poems* (Columbia University Press, 2000).

ABOUT THE AUTHOR

Fiona Sze-Lorrain writes and translates in English, French, and Chinese. She is the author of five poetry collections, most recently *Rain in Plural* (Princeton, 2020) and *The Ruined Elegance* (Princeton, 2016), and fifteen books of translation. A finalist for the Los Angeles Times Book Prize and the Best Translated Book Award among other honors, she was a 2019–20 Abigail R. Cohen Fellow at the Columbia Institute for Ideas and Imagination. She lives in Paris and has performed as a zheng harpist.